BLA

'Nobody in children's writing
anything like thi

D0735553

'Taut, int
a rema   ng series.'

        oks for Keeps

'A relentless and brilliant page turner.'

'A

7-13   Book 3

'My

'Yet

'T

BLADE

FIRESTORM

BLADE

TIM BOWLER

OXFORD
UNIVERSITY PRESS

OXFORD
UNIVERSITY PRESS

Great Clarendon Street, Oxford OX2 6DP

Oxford University Press is a department of the University of Oxford.
It furthers the University's objective of excellence in research, scholarship,
and education by publishing worldwide in

Oxford   New York

Auckland   Cape Town   Dar es Salaam   Hong Kong   Karachi
Kuala Lumpur   Madrid   Melbourne   Mexico City   Nairobi
New Delhi   Shanghai   Taipei   Toronto

With offices in

Argentina   Austria   Brazil   Chile   Czech Republic   France   Greece
Guatemala   Hungary   Italy   Japan   Poland   Portugal   Singapore
South Korea   Switzerland   Thailand   Turkey   Ukraine   Vietnam

Oxford is a registered trade mark of Oxford University Press
in the UK and in certain other countries

British Library Cataloguing in Publication Data

Data available

ISBN: 978-0-19-276362-4

1 3 5 7 9 10 8 6 4 2

Printed in Great Britain

Paper used in the production of this book is a natural,
recyclable product made from wood grown in sustainable forests.
The manufacturing process conforms to the environmental
regulations of the country of origin.

For Rachel
with my love

1

WELCOME TO THE Big Beast. Welcome to Hell.

Check around you, Bigeyes. Early morning, November sun. Cute little street, cute little school, cute little kiddies trigging through the gate. The great capital waking up around us. Plum place, yeah?

Think again.

Cos it's all wrong. It's zipping you over. Everything you see, everything you feel. Come closer, Bigeyes, and listen good. This is big new grime. It's not like the old city, the one we just escaped from.

This is the Beast.

And I'll tell you something about him.

Something you got to know.

Makes no difference how much sun there is, how many dinky kids or spiced up people you can see waking and shaking their lives into gear. The Beast's not what you think. Not what anyone thinks.

I know what I'm talking about. I was born here. I grew up here. If you can call it growing up. But never mind that. I know the Beast, right? I know him like I know my own body. If you think I was brained up on the old city, that's nothing to what I know about the Beast.

You probably heard about the taxi drivers. How they know every single street in the city. They learn it, road by road, and they get tested on it. Like it's a qualification. Yeah, right. Is that meant to impress me?

Well, it doesn't. I knew all that gump by the time I was seven. Every lane, every street, every dronky little mews. All the places too. Hotels, clubs, theatres, cinemas, brothels, you name it. All the bollocky monuments. I got so bored knowing everything about the Beast I made up my own names for all the different places.

I got that kind of memory. I remember everything I want to remember. People, places, stories, numbers, whatever. You wouldn't believe the stuff I can remember. That's one of the things that's got me in trouble. But here's what's weird about the Beast.

I learnt all these things about him, then I found I was wrong. I didn't really know the Beast at all. Not like I thought I did. I just knew the names, and the places to hide. I know him better now. You bet I do. And you got to get cracked on him too, Bigeyes.

Cos there's stuff about the Beast you got to learn fast.

First up, he's not like the old city. The one we just left. She was big, yeah, but she's nothing to this guy. Second, the Beast's not even a city, not even a capital. Yeah, yeah, he's called both. In the tourist books.

He's got all the bung they blab about. Stations, parks, banks, businesses, stores, sights, all that shit. But he's got something else too. Something you won't find in the tourist books.

Another city.

And another, and another, and another.

Cos here's what most nebs don't know. We're not in a city. We're in ten cities rolled into one. More than ten. The Beast's a country all his own. And I'm not just talking about size, Bigeyes, how far he spreads out. I'm talking about layers. Cities within cities, lives within lives.

That's where the darkness comes from.

The cities you don't see.

The lives you don't see.

Trust me. I know.

But never mind that now. Cop a glint over the kids. Most of 'em in the playground but some still ripping in through the gate. Keep back, well back, and watch cute. Stay behind this van and peep round the edge.

OK, Bigeyes, got the kids? Got the main gate? Right, now check out the car parked down on the left, the flash grey one. And the guy sitting at the wheel. Smooth gobbo, shiny suit, sharp eyes.

See 'em moving? Can't, can you? That's cos he's cute and you're a dimp. Look again, Bigeyes. Look better. Got 'em now? The eyes? Still missing 'em, aren't you? Dungpot.

Never mind. Take it from me. They're moving. I know. How do I know? Cos he's like me. He knows how to watch. So we got to stay fizzed. For one very good reason.

The bastards know I'm here.

Back at the Beast, I mean. I'm not talking about this little street, or this gobbo. Jesus, if he knew what's going on, I might as well flip over now. But he doesn't. He's smart and he watches good, but he hasn't slammed me. And he won't, unless I dunk it big time.

He's like all the other grinks. Does what he's told, gets paid, goes home. Asks no questions. No, I'm not talking about him. I'm talking about the scumbos who tell him what to do, and the slimeheads above them. They're the ones who'll know I'm back at the Beast.

It's a simple equation.

They got Jaz and they know I'll come for her. Cos they know I care. Xennie slung that one when she blotched on me and Bex. So they'll know I won't wig it out of here and all they got to do is wait till I show.

And they're right. I've come back for Jaz. She's all I want. I don't give two bells what happens to me long as she gets away safe. But I'll tell you something, Bigeyes. If she's dead, there's something else I'll have.

My revenge.

That's right, Bigeyes.

I'm fighting back.

Only problem is what to do about Bex. I can't leave her and she's clogged onto me. She's still mad at me. When the police turned up at the old prof's house, she was splitting my ear so bad we nearly didn't get away.

But I got her down the stairs and out the back door, and we made it over the fields to the motorway. Don't ask me how we didn't get caught. It's been a day and a night of hitching and hiding.

But here we are.

Still together. She's locked onto me, Bigeyes, and I can't drop her. She wants Jaz back as bad as I do. Problem is, I work better on my own. If Bex chokes up—which she could do easy—she'll shunt us both.

Check over my shoulder.

No sign of her, thank Christ. Been blamming my head over the thought of her standing in the middle of the road, tramping my gig for everyone to see. Took all my licky to persuade her to stay out of sight while I sniff out this patch.

But she's done it. Can't say she hasn't. Just hope she's where I left her. Cos there's no betting she will be. OK, we better shift before those gobbos clap us.

Yeah, Bigeyes, you heard right. I said gobbos. Didn't see the second guy, did you? Over to the right, further down. Got him now? Beefcake, grey suit, leaning against the outside wall of the playground.

Let's get out of here.

2

BACK DOWN THE street, keeping behind the parked cars. Check about you, Bigeyes, check good. Cos everywhere we go now, we got to keep out of sight and watch cute. We got to see the shit before the shit sees us.

There's more dangers in the Beast than in the old city. She was bad but this bastard's got eyes everywhere. Down to the bottom of the street, check round, check again, through the park, past the tube, into the alleyway.

Stop, check the street behind. All clear. Down the alleyway, follow the bend round, up to the wall at the end.

And there's Bex.

Slumped on the ground behind the big dustbin. Just where I left her. I breathe slowly out. Thought she might have wigged it. And that'd be bad, Bigeyes. The grinks'd chew her up in five minutes if she cut off on her own.

She looks up, accusing.

'Didn't think you'd come back,' she sulks.

'I told you I would.'

'Yeah.' She sniffs. 'You done.'

'Meaning what?'

'Meaning your word ain't worth shit.'

'I've stuck with you. All the way here. I could have cleared off any time I wanted.'

'Whatever.'

She looks away, looks back.

'Ain't only me, is it?' she gripes. 'Not trusting.'

'I don't know what you're talking about.'

I do, Bigeyes. But never mind that.

'You don't trust me neither,' she goes on. 'I can see it in your face. I watched you coming down the alleyway. You was thinking I bet that slag's pissed off.'

'I don't think you're a slag.'

'But you was thinking I'd pissed off.'

I shrug.

'Whatever.'

She bursts into tears. First time she's blubbed since we scraped it out the old prof's house. She was all tears in there, and I don't blame her. Dig murdered, Jaz taken, all the grime. But since we got away she's gone quiet. She's still blazing at me—I can feel that—but it's from the inside. Like a weird, silent anger. No words, no frowns, no punches or slaps.

And no tears.

Till now. But maybe that's best. She's got a lot of stuff inside her.

Like me.

Only difference is I'm not crying. And you know why, Bigeyes? Cos I won't let myself. I've told myself no tears till I get Jaz back. I got to be strong for that kid.

Bex goes on blubbing.

I sit down next to her, let her bawl. She takes no notice of me. It's a few minutes before she's quiet again. Just sits there, wet eyes, half-open. She's gone into herself again. Then suddenly she turns her head, fixes me.

'You got to talk,' she says.

I look at her. She's not just angry now. She's close to breaking up. I can see it in her face. And there's something else, Bigeyes. She's right. I owe her some words.

And anyway, she needs to know a bit.

Not all of it. Not sure I can tell all of it. But some of it. If only so she knows how dangerous things are. But I guess she's clapped that already.

'That guy in the house,' she mutters. 'The one what said tell Blade if he wants the little girl back, he knows where to come.'

'What about him?'

'Was he right?'

'Maybe.'

'Maybe?' She grabs me by the collar, thrusts her face close. 'Maybe?'

'Bex—'

'Was he right, yes or no?'

'He was right.'

'You shit!'

She pushes me away.

'Bex—'

'Shut it!'

'Bex—'

'I said shut it!'

I'm thinking hard, Bigeyes. How to do this. She wants me to talk but she's too angry to listen. I got to get her back on my side or we're spiked. I jump up, reach out a hand.

'Come here, Bex.'

She looks up at me like I got a disease.

'I don't need your frigging hand to get up.'

She climbs to her feet by herself. She's swaying, still bombed, still choked.

'So what you got for me now?' she grumps. 'More lies?'

'I want to show you something.'

I don't wait for her, just walk back down the alleyway. I can hear her following. More of a waddle than a walk but she's coming. Round the bend, on to the end of the alleyway, stop, check round into the street.

Looks cute. But I'm wary.

Bex catches up, stops by my shoulder.

'Where we going?' she mutters.

'Nowhere.'

'So what you wasting my time for?'

'Look over the road.'

She's quiet for a moment. I don't check if she's watching. I know she is. I can feel it.

'What's so special?' she says suddenly.

'Tell me what you see. Over the road.'

'Houses.'

'Look again. Left to right. Tell me what you see.'

She gives a sigh.

'Go on,' I say.

'House, house, house, house,' she goes, bored voice, 'house, empty space, house—'

'Stop.'

'What?'

'Look at the empty space.'

Another silence. Again I don't check. Again I feel her looking. At more than one thing too. Don't ask me how I know. But I can feel it. She's looking at the empty space. And she's looking at me too. I can feel her eyes moving from one to the other.

But I'm just looking at one thing.

She speaks, spitty now.

'You going to tell me what this is about?'

'It's not an empty space.'

'What?'

I look round at her this time.

'It's not an empty space.'

She glowers at me, stares back over the road, shrugs.

'All right, it's a car park. Only it's got no cars in it. So it's an empty space. Far as I'm concerned.'

'It's where I first lived.'

I got her attention now. She narrows her eyes.

'You lived in a car park?'

'It wasn't a car park then.'

'What was it?'

'A home.'

She leans out into the street to get a better look. I yank her back into the alleyway.

'Don't,' I say.

'There's nobody watching.'

'There's always somebody watching.'

'Let go of me,' she snarls.

I let go. She stays where she is, flicks her eyes over the road, fixes 'em back on me.

'What kind of a home?' she says.

'A shit home.'

I look over the road. And you know what, Bigeyes? It's weird. Like that other place is still there. Like it'll always be there. Like you could smash away all the houses, clear the rubble out, turn the whole effing street into one great globby piece of nothing, and you know what?

That part of it still won't be an empty space.

Cos ghosts don't leave that easy. And this one's still there. I can feel it.

'They found me outside the door,' I murmur.

Bex is quiet. But I can feel her waiting.

'I was in a box,' I say. 'So they told me later. Might all be lies. Just making up a story. Baby in a box. Kind of romantic, yeah? Long as you're not the bloody baby. But that's what they told me. Said I got left there by whoever my parents were. Or somebody else maybe. Christ knows. But they took me in, the people who worked there, gave me a name.'

'What was it?'

'Never mind. And that's where I first lived.'

'How long for?'

'Four years. Then I got moved on.'

'You *got* moved on?'

'Yeah.'

Bex is quiet again. But I know the question she's going to ask next. And here it comes, clipping into my head.

'What was it like, this home?'

I don't answer. I can't suddenly. I got flashbacks hitting me again. Same ones I always get when I think of this place. Memories without faces, memories without shapes. Not even memories really. Just the feeling of 'em, the fear of 'em.

The pain.

I look at her. I can feel tears pushing up, spite of what I said about not crying. I hold 'em back, just, but I'm struggling and Bex has picked it up. I can tell from the way she's fixing me. She bites her lip, looks away.

A car draws up in the street. We both pull back. I check out. Dronky old motor turning into the car park, ancient gobbo driving. Little kid on the front seat. His grandson, I'm guessing. Same mouth and nose.

They get out, gobbo buys a parking ticket, they trig off down the street. Kid looks about four. Could have been me all those years ago. Same colour hair even.

Bex speaks again.

'What happened to the home?'

I look round at her.

'I burnt it down.'

3

'JESUS!' SHE SAYS.

She sticks her head out again to get a better look. I pull her back into the alleyway.

'Stay out of sight.'

'There's nobody,' she says. 'I just told you.'

'Stay back.'

You too, Bigeyes. Cos there's something she hasn't seen, something you haven't seen. A car chunking down from the right. It's not the one those gobbos had down by the school. It's a bigger one.

'Can't see nobody,' says Bex.

'Stay back.'

'Let go my arm.'

Didn't realize I was still holding her. I let go, but I'm watching her cute, like I'm watching the street cute. Can't see the car now. We're too far into the alleyway. But I can feel it.

'Keep back,' I say.

Sound of voices coming close. Nothing to do with the car. Women talking, loud and snappy. We'll see 'em in a moment and they'll see us. Just hope they don't blotch us to the nebs in the car. Cos I'll tell you something, Bigeyes. It's not muffins in that thing.

Don't ask me how I know.

Two dolls, twenties, triked up with lippy, naffing their mouths off. They stop in the opening, see us, fall quiet.

'How you doing?' I call.

'Who the hell are you?' says one.

'Man from the moon,' says the other. 'And his bird.'

Both snigger. But I'm watching the street past their shoulders. Car's stopped. I can see the bonnet. Black motor, engine snorting.

'We got to go,' I say.

'Something we said?' snipes the first woman.

She cackles and her mate joins in. Sound of a car door, another. I grab Bex by the arm.

'Come on.'

'Blade—'

'Come on!'

I pull her down the alleyway, but she's holding back.

'Bex, come on!'

The women go on laughing.

'Bex! We got to run! And we can't go back to the street!'

'But this alleyway don't go nowhere. It's a dead end.'

'Just do what I do!'

Sound of hard, gruff voices. Now Bex starts to run. More voices, the women arguing with the gobbos, spluttering, squealing. Sound of a slap, screams, then footsteps thundering after us.

'Come on, Bex!'

We race down the alleyway, round the bend, stop at the far wall. Check behind. No sign of 'em yet. But they'll be here any second.

'What now?' says Bex.

'Over the wall. There's a little courtyard on the other side. Back of a shoe shop.'

'How do you know?'

'Never mind. Just climb over the wall and run like shit.'

'But it's too high!'

'Get on the dustbin!'

She clambers up and over. I'm straight after her, just in time. Gobbos storm in as I drop down the other side. We hare round the shop and out into the street. Bex turns left. I catch her arm.

'Other way.'

She doesn't argue. We sprint off, both panting. Check over my shoulder. The gobbos'll hit the street any moment. We got to be quick.

'Left here, Bex.'

Past the bank, over the car park, through the bike sheds, down the path, over the fence into the allotment, down to the far end, over the other fence, up to the main road, check behind.

Three gobbos pounding after us. They must have gone

the other way to start with, like I hoped they would, so we bought a few seconds. But not many. They're coming on fast.

'What do we do?' says Bex.

I can hear the terror in her voice. I check the road, walk off the kerb, hold out a hand, scream.

'Taxi!'

It pulls over. Bex runs up and joins me. I pull open the door.

'Get in, Bex.'

We pile in the back. I glance at the allotment. Gobbos close to the fence now. If the driver doesn't pull out soon, they'll block the motor and we're done. I look at him. He's turned round and he's fixing us slow, like he's wondering if he made a mistake picking us up.

'Let's go, mate,' I say.

'Where to?' he glums.

'Over the river. I'll tell you where to stop.'

'You got money?'

'Yeah, no problem.'

I feel Bex grab my arm. She's staring at the gobbos sliming close and she's choking up bad. I got to act quick or she'll freeze the driver.

'I got money, mate. It's not a problem. Other side of the river. That's cool.'

He's still not convinced. Bex's hand clamps me hard. I see the grinks spread out. They're walking now, so they don't look suspicious, but they're moving fast and one's cutting into the road to block the taxi. Driver hasn't seen 'em yet. I give him a nod.

'Let's go, mate.' I glance at Bex, give her a peck on the cheek. 'All right, babe?'

She doesn't speak, just clings on. Driver's looking her over. This isn't working. I got to try something else. I lean forward, stare past him.

'Who the hell's that?' I say.

Driver turns, sees the grink in front of the taxi. Gestures at him.

'Move it!'

Grink stays put.

'Get out the way!' shouts the driver.

Grink starts to edge forward. Other gobbos step closer. Hard men, all of 'em. We can't handle this crew. And the driver's not going to help us. But I'm wrong. He twists round, winds down the window, sticks his head out.

'Get out the bloody way!'

Then he ramps up the revs, pulls out and suddenly we're round 'em, tanking down the road. He spits out the window, closes it, glances round. But he's not checking me and Bex. He's checking the grinks. He watches for a moment, then turns back to his driving.

'I've had it up to here today,' he mutters. 'Wanky drivers, wanky passengers, wanky jay-walkers.'

Glances round again. And this time he's looking at me.

'You better have that money on you.'

'I got it.'

'Show me.'

I see the fear back in Bex's face, feel her hand clamp

me again. Gobbo's still checking me. He's turned back to his driving but he's watching in the mirror. I reach into my pocket, pull out a note.

Bex's eyes widen, but she doesn't speak.

I hold up the money for the driver to see. He gives a shrug.

'Fair enough.'

'Happy now?'

'Where'd you say you want to go?'

'Over the river.'

'Then what?'

'I'll tell you when we get there.'

He says nothing. But I can feel him still watching us. We got to make this a short ride. The grinks'll have his registration number going round by now. Bex lets go of my arm, leans back. I glance at her.

She's breathing hard, really hard. She's not going to last, Bigeyes. I'm telling you. She's never going to last. Not in the Beast. She's wiped in her head. Don't ask me what I'm going to do about it. Cos I don't know.

Check out the window.

Yeah, right. See that, Bigeyes? The bastard sights. Some of 'em anyway. There's loads more, if you like that kind of thing. But here's a fistload in one plug. Tourists pay big jippy to see this. Christ knows why. And here's the worst bit coming up.

Mother Grime.

Bitch of a river. Don't give two bells how famous it is, how much history it's got, how many songs and poems and cranky paintings they've done of it. All I know is it's wide and it's deep and it's wet, and I wish we didn't have to cross it.

'Which bridge?' says the driver.

'Next one.'

I catch his eyes in the mirror again. He's not angry like he was, but he's curious. He doesn't know what to make of us. And he's starting to chew over those gobbos. He thought they were nothing to do with us. But now he's wondering.

Bex is wondering too. I can see it in her face. But she's not wondering about the gobbos. She's trying to work out how come I got money. Well, she'll have to go on wondering, and so can you. Cos I can't talk now. I got to keep fixed on the driver.

He's turned onto the first bridge. Bogeybum I call it. Don't ask me why. I've just always called it that. Yeah, I know. You're confused. Well, I don't care. I told you. I got my own names for the places in the Beast. Get over it.

I got to focus on what I'm doing.

Halfway across. I'm watching cute now, checking cars, faces, and Mother Grime slinking underneath us. God, I hate this river. Don't feel safe, even in a taxi on Bogeybum Bridge. But we're nearly over. And then we got to split.

Fast.

Just a bit further. Wait, wait, wait. Driver's watching me in the mirror again. I take no notice, check round, check again, call out.

'Pull over.'

4

HE PULLS OVER, checks the meter, looks round.
I don't wait for him to speak, just pass him the note.

'Keep the change.'

He raises an eyebrow.

'You serious?'

'Keep it.' I nod to Bex. 'Let's go.'

We climb out. Driver's watching us, frowning. I give
him a wave. He goes on watching, then slowly pulls out
from the kerb. But he's on his mobile straightaway.

'Come on, Bex.'

'Which way?'

'North side of the river.'

'We just come from there.'

'I want to get back. I don't trust the driver. He's ringing
a mate or the police. And the other lot could get hold of
him. I got to make 'em all think we're on the south side.
Come on.'

She doesn't move, just stands there, trembling.

'Bex, come on.'

It's no good. She's blanked up. I don't blame her. She's blasted over Dig and Jaz, choked up to her head with all that's happening. But I got to shift her and I got to do it quick, cos we're stuck here in full view of every grink who slimes up.

I take her arm, talk soft as I can.

'Bex, listen. We got to get off the road, keep out of sight. Got to do it for Jaz.'

She still doesn't move. Jesus, Bigeyes, I don't know what to do. She's just blobbed there. Got to think of something. I lean forward, give her another kiss on the cheek. She jerks back like I slapped her.

'Stop doing that!'

Pushes my hand off her arm.

'And don't ever call me babe again.'

She fixes me.

'*Which way?*'

I don't answer, just lead her to the side of the road, down the steps, under the bridge. I don't check to see if she's following. I can feel she is. And anyway, I got to watch elsewhere. Cute as I can.

No sign of danger under the bridge. Couple of duffs curled on the ground. Kids on rollerblades rippling past. Out the other side of the bridge, cut left, cut right, on down the road.

Check behind.

She's still there, scowling at me. I want to help her,

Bigeyes. I know you don't believe me but I do. I feel responsible. I am responsible. She's right to be angry. If it weren't for me, the grinks wouldn't have taken Jaz.

Wouldn't have murdered Dig.

Or Trixi. They were looking for me in the bungalow, remember.

So it's my fault. Like so many other things. I don't blame Bex for hating me. I hate myself too. But I got to get past this. Got to make my hatred do some good. Got to save it for the grinks. Or there's no point fighting back.

Won't change Bex's feelings about me. Whatever I do, she's going to rage. But I can't let myself care about it too much. Got to focus on what I can do, not what I can't. Funny though, what she said about me kissing her.

I mean, think about it, Bigeyes. Couldn't she see I was acting the first time? And just trying to help her the second? Christ's sake, like I'm ever going to want to kiss her, even on the cheek.

She speaks suddenly. 'Blade.'

Different voice. Still angry but something else too. Sadness, despair, can't tell. I look round. She's stopped, middle of the pavement, and she's crying. I walk back to her. Don't know what to do. She goes on whacking out tears. 'Bex, we can't stop here.'

She looks me in the face, stares hard for a moment, then pushes past and heads on up the road. But she's walking blind. I can tell. She's just . . . tramping on. Not watching, not seeing, not caring. I catch her up, take her arm.

'Bex, not that way.'

She stops.

'It's where you was heading,' she mutters.

'We got to cut down here.'

I point to the right. She glances that way, sniffs.

'Another alleyway.'

'Yeah.'

'So that's it, is it?' She wipes her eyes with her sleeve. 'Where we're going to be living from now on. Alleyways.'

'We got to stay out of sight.'

'Yeah, yeah.'

'We can't take the big streets, Bex. There's too many people watching. Even the alleyways are dangerous. Cos they know we'll be using 'em.'

'Not much point then, is there?' She glowers at me. 'Might as well give up on Jaz now. Cos you ain't going to do nothing. You know where she is. But all you're going to do is creep round alleyways. Till they catch us.'

'Bex—'

She turns away, plods down the alleyway. I check round, check again, follow. She's trigging slow, shoulders hunched. I feel so bad now, Bigeyes. I got a plan, got an idea what I can do, but it's so risky, so hard to crack, and harder still with Bex in tow. Specially when she's like this.

She stops suddenly, turns.

'You're shit, Blade. If I knew where Jaz was, I'd go straight there.'

'Yeah, you would.' I fix her. 'Cos you're stupid enough to think that would work.'

She slaps me hard in the face. I wince, but don't move. Didn't see it coming, but I see the next one. Other hand, whipping in. I let her hit me, and again, and again. She's still crying, great sobby tears, and she's lashing out big time, hard, heavy slaps, like she wants to split my face.

I stand there, take it, then suddenly she stops, half-falls over me, chin on my shoulder, arms loose.

'You bastard,' she mutters. 'I hate you so much.'

'I know you do.'

She doesn't answer, just stays there, flopped against me.

'Bex, listen . . .'

She starts to whimper. She's still got her arms hanging loose, her chin dug into my shoulder. I hesitate, put an arm round her, wait for her to pull back, spit, slap, whatever. She doesn't do anything, just stays like she is.

I check round us. Got to keep doing that, Bigeyes, whatever's going on with Bex. Nobody in the alleyway. Flick a glance back at the street. Nebs passing by, all muffins so far. But we can't stay here long. Got to wig it off the south side before the grinks snap in.

'Bex . . .'

She shrugs my arm off her, pulls back. I try and fix her. She won't let me, just stares down at the ground.

'Bex, I'm in it for Jaz, OK?'

She doesn't answer.

'I'm in it for Jaz,' I say. 'Like you. But I can't just walk in there.'

She lifts her eyes, glimmy with tears.

'They wants you,' she mumbles. 'Them guys. I don't know who they is. And I don't know what you done, cos you ain't saying nothing. But I know they wants you. And they don't want Jaz. So it's easy.'

'It's not.'

'It is.'

She leans closer.

'You give yourself up. And Jaz goes free.'

She pauses.

'And before you ask—no, I don't care what they do to you.'

I shove past her, stomp down the alleyway. She calls after me.

'But you ain't going to help her, are you? Cos like I say, you're shit!'

I stop, clench my fists. OK, that's it. She wants to bomb words? So do I. I turn, drill the troll—then catch a movement behind her. Higher than the street, higher than the roofs of the houses. Up on the bridge where the taxi dropped us off.

Two gobbos checking round.

Might not be grinks.

But I got a bad feeling about 'em.

'Bex, we got to go.'

'Yeah, yeah,' she whines, 'we got to go. We always got to go. Find another alleyway, find another excuse.'

From up on the bridge comes a shout.

'There!'

One of the gobbos is pointing at us. Bex turns, sees him, looks at me. And the terror's back in her face.

'Come on!' I yell.

5 SHE DOESN'T ARGUE this time. She's sprinting down the alleyway so fast I can't keep up with her. I let her race ahead. Doesn't matter, long as I can see her. She's running blind, like she was walking blind a moment ago, not seeing, not thinking.

But I'm doing both.

Checking the dark corners, the places to watch, and thinking, even as I run. Alleyway cuts into a side street just ahead, and then we got choices. Not many and they're all bad, but we got a chance.

Can't run our way out of this. There'll be grinks crowding the area in minutes. And we'll never hike another taxi cos they don't come down these streets much. So it's hook a smelly or hit the snakehole.

Both crappy options.

Plenty of smellies rumbling about. Number 49 goes over the next bridge and there's a stop round the corner.

Trouble is—what's the chance of one turning up just when we need it? Not much. We'll run past the stop but it's a long shot.

Which case we'll have to smack it with the snakehole.

But that's even more dangerous. They'll have dronks watching all the stations. Got no choice though. It's get away or get caught. And we might just slip through if we play it cute.

'Bex!'

She's still tearing ahead.

'Bex! Cut left at the end. But check it's clear first.'

She doesn't check, just cuts left and disappears from view. Crazy troll. She's got no idea. She's got to think what she's doing, even though she's scared. She could be running straight into 'em. I'm praying they're not waiting for her round the bend.

We'll soon find out.

End of the alleyway, stop, check behind.

No sign of the gobbos from the bridge. Check into the street. No grinks in sight, just a couple of workmen digging up the road, and Bex pelting on. Bloody hell, Bigeyes, I got to haul her back somehow.

Trouble is, I don't want to shout. Draws attention. But wait a sec. She's stopping by herself. Turns, stares back at me. She looks like a hunted deer. I run down to her, hoping she won't bundle off again.

She doesn't, just stands there, gasping. I catch the workmen looking, flick 'em a smile, make like it's no bum gripe. They don't smile back. And they don't look away either. I ease Bex off to the left.

'Where we going?' she moans.

'Bus stop.'

'Bus stop?'

'Yeah.'

But it's like I told you, Bigeyes. Not a smelly in sight.

'OK, Bex, this way.'

I pull her into the next street.

'Now where we going?' she mutters.

'Just follow, OK? Cut the shit. We're surrounded and we've only got minutes to do this.'

'Do what?'

'Catch the tube.'

She stares at me.

'You got money for it?'

'Yeah.'

'How come? You didn't hardly have no money when we ran away. So you said. And then you pulls out a note for the taxi driver and—'

'Shut it, can you?'

I'm checking round as we walk, checking cute.

'I haven't got time for this, OK? We got to shift. Just do what I say. I'll tell you about the money later.'

She shuts up, thank Christ.

We walk on, fast. I want to run but it's a bad idea now. Too obvious, specially if there's eyes round the tube station. Least the day's getting busy. I'm hoping there'll be a good crowd hitting the snakehole. If there is, we might just snick in among 'em.

Right at the end of the street, down to the bottom, check round. Next bridge getting closer, nebs swarming round it. Hard to tell who's a muffin and who's a grink. And that's not all. We got porkers to think about too. Don't forget them.

No sign of any yet but they won't be far.

Cut right, away from the bridge. Keep to the side of the road. Cars sniffing past. Check out the carriageway. Might just be lucky with a taxi, but I doubt it. They don't usually like this road cos it's hard to pull over with the bus lane.

Here's the tube station. Left, down the lane behind the sandwich bar, out the other side, check over the road. Good—lots of nebs trigging down the steps into the snakehole. Nice muffiny-looking nebs too. One or two dronks hanging out either side of the entrance but they look more like duffs than grinks.

Walk on, slow, stop behind the refuse van.

Bex bumps into me from behind. I round on her.

'Watch what you're doing.'

'You stopped sudden,' she grumbles.

I fix her, wait for her to fix me back.

'This is serious, Bex.'

'I know.'

'Then do what I say.'

I wait. Her eyes have wandered off again. They look so scared. I can't find the heart to bollock her like I should.

'Bex?'

'What?'

'Do exactly what I say, OK?'

She shrugs.

'OK.'

'You don't walk with me. You don't talk to me. You don't look at me. You check me out now and again. But casual, yeah? Not so anyone can see you do it. We mustn't look like we're together. Can you do all that?'

'I'm not an idiot.'

'It's important, Bex. OK? Keep apart from me all the time. I'll get the tickets. Just follow me, get on the same train, sit apart.'

I reach into my pocket, pull out some coins.

'There'll be a newspaper stand on the platform.'

'How do you know?'

'Never mind. Buy a magazine. When you're sitting down, pretend you're reading it. Cover your face as much as you can. Only don't make like you're trying to do it. You know what I mean?'

'I just told you. I'm not an idiot.'

'And don't catch anyone's eye. Or look up at any cameras.'

'Can we just go?'

I check round again. It all looks plum. That's what bothers me. I walk up to the kerb, stop. Feel Bex move up behind me. Jesus Christ, she's forgotten what I said already. I don't look round, just mutter over my shoulder.

'Stay back. You're too close.'

Feel her start to edge away. I mutter again.

'No, don't move back now. You'll make it too obvious. Just let me get ahead, then follow. Keep some distance between us. Like I say, I'll get both tickets. I'll leave yours where you can pick it up. So watch close so you don't miss it. Let's go.'

Can't wait any longer, Bigeyes. It's now or never.

6 BUT THERE'S ALREADY four new gobbos hanging round the entrance to the station. They might not be trouble and we still got to try. But I'm less confident than I was ten seconds ago.

And I wasn't confident then.

Over the road, slopey walk, eyes down. Bex hasn't followed. I can feel that without looking. She's hanging back like I told her to. Least she's got that bit right. Just hope she starts walking soon. She's leaving it a bit long.

Check back.

Here she comes. Slow walk, like me. Turn back to the entrance. Time to brisk up. If there's grinks here, they'll block us straight off. They won't let us hit the steps. But we might just have got here first.

Two gobbos to the right. Don't like the look of 'em. They don't stop me but they're checking behind me, maybe watching Bex. I chuck her another glance. Still crossing the road after me. Doesn't catch my eye.

Good girl.

Keep doing that.

Into the entrance, and no one's stopped me. Over to the ticket machine, money in, snap the tickets, over to the barrier, check behind. She's a little way back, further than I want her to be, but there's no one between us. Just hope she claps this.

I drop to my knee, fiddle with a shoelace, leave one ticket on the ground, straighten up, walk through the barrier, on towards the escalator. Check behind, and there's Bex through the barrier, coming on too.

Down the escalator, through the tunnel, onto the platform. Check the sign. Train coming in two minutes. Bex appears, takes no notice of me, walks past, buys a newspaper from the stand, waits further down the platform.

Two gobbos trig up, the ones I saw earlier. They walk on, stop between me and Bex. She flicks open the newspaper, buries her face in it. She's bummed this one, Bigeyes. Should have bought a magazine like I told her to. She doesn't look right holding a newspaper, specially that one.

If she'd got a tabloid, it wouldn't be so bad. But she's bought a heavyweight bloody broadsheet. Who's going to believe she reads that thing for fun? I know why she got it. Cos it's big. Cos it covers her face. But she didn't think. Jesus! She couldn't stand out more if she tried.

Both gobbos are looking at her.

But here comes the train.

She hears it, shakes down the newspaper, folds it up, checks my way. Train pulls in, stops, doors open, nebs pile off. I wait for the gobbos to move. They don't, just stand there, talking. I feel Bex watching me again.

I walk up to the door, wait for the gobbos again. They move up to the next door, stop. I step on the train. They do the same. Bex climbs on. Same door as the two guys. Walks to the end of the carriage, sits down, flicks open the newspaper again.

Gobbos walk over to her, stand nearby. I walk down the other end, find a spot, sit down. Doors close, train rattles off. Check round. Carriage half full. Muffins, no question, apart from the two gobbos.

Can't make up my mind about 'em. Got to play this cute, got to watch without watching, fix their shadows and get ready to cop their spit if they make a move on Bex. Don't think she's even noticed 'em. She's got the newspaper over her face again.

Train clatters on, pulls into the next station.

I get up, walk down the carriage to the middle doors. The gobbos are still at the end, close to Bex. I can see her watching me over the top of the newspaper. I take no notice of her, stand by the door, wait for the train to stop.

It slows down, judders, comes to a halt.

Bex stands up, folds up the newspaper, edges past the gobbos.

Doors open.

I get off, walk down the platform past Bex's door, feel her slip behind me. Check over my shoulder. Gobbos are climbing off too. I walk on, waiting, watching.

Jump back on the train, next carriage.

Bex does the same.

Doors close. Train moves off. No sign of the gobbos but there's panic in Bex's face. It's freezing her up, all this. She starts to walk over. I turn away. Mustn't let her talk to me. She's got to stay cool or we're goosed. The gobbos aren't in this carriage but that means nothing. They could easily have got back on the train.

And if they did, we'll know they're trouble.

I don't sit down. Plenty of spaces but I walk past 'em all to the end of the carriage. Turn round. Bloody Christ! Bex is still walking towards me. I turn my head, sharp as I can. But I can still feel her coming on.

What's wrong with this troll? She's got to pick up signals. Even if she's freaked, she's got to pick up signals and act her part. I turn my back to her and hold on, swinging with the train. She steps alongside me.

'Go away,' I mutter.

'I'm scared, Blade.'

Her voice is so small. Makes me think of Jaz. I glance at her. She's gone right inside herself. Eyes blank, like she's folding up. I mustn't let her do this. Those gobbos could well be on the train. And even if they aren't, there's still grinks all around us.

I take my eyes off her. Got to play my part, whatever

she's feeling. Got to act like we're not together. But I can feel her trembling now. She's leaning against me and she's shaking. I murmur to her.

'It's all right, Bex.'

'I'm so . . . I'm so . . . '

'It's all right. I won't let anyone hurt you.'

I feel her body press against mine. She's still shaking. Train pulls into the next station.

'Are we getting off?' she breathes.

'Don't know yet.'

I check the carriage, edge towards the door. Feel Bex take my hand, squeeze it. I don't look at her. It's no good. I got to check things super-cute here. Only I can't let go of her hand. I should do. I know I should. Cos this is madness. But I can't make myself. For her sake. Didn't think I'd ever say that.

She squeezes my hand again.

'It's all right, Bex. It's all right.'

Doors open.

I lean out, check the station. No sign of the two guys. But there's three other gobbos on the platform. Just standing there, watching the faces of the nebs getting off. I don't trust 'em. Whip my head back inside the train.

'We're staying on, Bex.'

She says nothing, just goes on holding my hand. Nebs piling into the carriage now. I look round at Bex, give her hand a squeeze, then slip mine free. Lean close, whisper.

'Go and sit down there. Have another read of the newspaper.'

She's not going to do it, Bigeyes. Look at her face. She's so choked up she'll never move. But I'm wrong. She glances at me, same empty eyes, then walks down the carriage, sits where I told her, opens the newspaper.

I'm tense as a spring now. Check up and down the carriage. It's almost full. Only one space left, opposite Bex. Might as well take it. Better than standing here. Can't be seen so easy.

I walk over, check round, sit down. Just hope Bex keeps her head and doesn't talk or anything. Glance at her. She's got the newspaper open and she's holding it so high I can't see her face. But I can see another face. On the front page. A photo.

Of me.

Age eleven.

And a headline.

WHO IS BLADE?

7

I DON'T SUPPOSE BEX has seen it. She'd be reading the article otherwise. I lean forward, couple of inches. Hard to see clear but I can scrape most of the words.

It's like I suspected. Porkers have rounded up the gang. Xen probably cracked her mouth. I'm guessing conscience hit her. Or the trolls did. Someone needed to. Anyway, they're in custody. Tammy, Sash, Xen, Kat.

No mention of Riff. What a surprise. He's probably dribbled under a stone, hoping the trolls'll lick the swill for him. Makes no difference. The talking's started, the name Blade's out there, plus my old police photo, and it's a big, big story.

First the body count. Trixi and Dig. The gobbo in the hospital, the dunny in the snug. Paddy, Lenny, and the grunt. No details about the grinks. Probably cos the porkers can't work out who they are.

Then the other stuff.

Bex and Jaz still missing. Gob from the gang about what happened at the old prof's house. Witness report from 'an elderly Irish woman who befriended the boy'. Bless her sweet, beautiful heart.

Then the speculation.

Who is Blade?

And you know what, Bigeyes? That's how it's always been. Who is Blade? Cos here's the thing. No one knows. Some nebs think they do but they're wrong. I'd had a hundred names by the time I was ten and Blade was just another.

You want to know who Blade is?

I'll tell you.

I'm whoever you want me to be.

I'm a story you make up for yourself.

To the trolls, I'm a kid who pissed on their turf. To the other nebs in the old city, the few I let near me, I'm whatever name I gave 'em. And it wasn't Blade. So to them I don't exist.

Different in the Beast. Cos the name came from here. From Becky originally. But by the time I ran away, it was all anyone called me. Porkers, grinks, gangs. They all knew the name. And they all thought they knew me.

But I'll say it again.

I'm whoever you want me to be.

The newspaper says I'm a fourteen-year-old boy who's been in trouble with the police all his life. A kid who's been missing for the last three years, who's dangerous with a knife. A kid who might have killed.

Now read the last sentence of the article. Go on. Read what it says.

Who is Blade?

You see? They still don't know.

But I'm not the only story on the front page.

MARKETS IN TURMOIL AS GLOBAL CRISIS DEEPENS.

Yeah, right. Is that supposed to be news? Well, it's not to me. I could have told you years ago this was going to happen. Business hitting the grime. Economies round the world getting blasted. Don't believe me? Well, I don't care. I knew it was coming.

Cos I know some of the bastards behind it. Trust me, it's not just greedy bankers grubbing the patch. They're part of it, yeah, but there's more to it than just them. The real slime's somewhere else, somewhere nobody's looking.

The storm's breaking, Bigeyes.

So you better get ready.

Train rumbles on through the snakehole.

Bex lowers the newspaper, catches my eye, looks away. I stand up, edge towards the door, feel her do the same behind me. Train shivers into the next station, slows down, stops. Doors open.

I check out. Looks clear.

Onto the platform, Bex just behind. She's left the paper on the train. Into the tunnel, up the escalator, through the barrier, up the steps towards the street. Bex starts to catch me up.

I stop, nod her back.

She stays where she is. I walk on, slow. Got to check the exit, make sure it's cute. Lots of nebs busying about, but I can't see any danger. Doesn't mean much. The biggest danger's always the one you never see.

Glance round. Bex is still standing where she was. I turn, slip out into the street, cut right, check behind. She's following, keeping back like before. Long as she stays like that, we're plum.

Trouble is, she probably won't.

And even if she does, I got to keep checking her.

So you might as well know, Bigeyes. I've made my mind up about something. It means using someone from the past, someone I've been trying to keep out of this, and it'll be a tough gripe. I'm not happy about it at all.

But I got to try.

Cos to put it bluntly, I can't drag Bex much further.

First up, she's dronky at doing this. Ducking, dodging, kissing shadows. She'll shunt us both if we carry on like this. And second, she'll never slam what I got to do tomorrow. No way. She'll hate it so much she'll try and stop me.

Maybe you will too.

Cos I'm telling you, Bigeyes, you won't like it either.

But it's something I got to do, OK? It's for the best. Only Bex won't see that. Like I say, she'll try and stop me. And I can't have her crabbing my gut. Or you. So remember that, Bigeyes. I'm giving you fair warning.

Keep your distance when tomorrow comes. You'll know when I'm squeezing the flame. Cos you'll hate what you're seeing. But get in my way and you're dust. Anyway, that's for later. First things first.

Round the corner, hugging the wall. Keep close to the offices. Twisty little street. Nebs everywhere, jacking the pubs and sandwich bars. We better get some food ourselves. Haven't eaten for hours and I can't believe Bex hasn't guffed about it yet.

But we got to hit another place first. If it hasn't closed down in the three years I've been away from the Beast. Jesus, it's still there. See it? The old charity shop. Crappy as ever.

Check it out, Bigeyes. Would you want to buy from a place like that? Even for charity? Just as well I only want two things. Stop outside, check round. Bex is hovering a short way back.

I nod her towards the doorway on her right. She slinks into it, but sticks her head out and fixes me.

'Wait in there,' I mouth.

She disappears.

No problem in the shop. Two minutes and I'm out again. Down the street to the doorway and there's Bex, looking scared. She stiffens at the sight of me and I got a feeling she's been crying again. But she speaks.

'What you got in that bag?'

'Two big coats. With hoods. What colour do you want?'

'Neither.'

'Take one.'

'I like what I got.'

'Take one. Pull it over what you got. Should be big enough.'

'What for?'

Jesus, Bigeyes. I can't believe she just asked me that.

'We got to keep changing our appearance, Bex. Come on. Choose one.'

She checks in the bag.

'Shit colours,' she says.

'They're meant to be. I want 'em boring. So they don't stand out.'

She sniffs.

'I'll have the brown one.'

I check round, make sure no one's watching, pass her the coat. She puts it on, frowning.

'You paid for this?'

'Yeah.'

'What with?'

I don't answer, just pull the grey coat out the bag, rip off my old coat.

'Ain't you keeping that?' says Bex.

'No.'

I turn my back to her, swap the jippy from my old pockets to the new ones. But she sees.

'You bastard,' she mutters. 'You got great frigging wodges of money. Where'd you get all that?'

'Tell you later.'

'Tell me now.'

'I'll tell you later. We got to go. Come on.'

She grabs me by the arm, snarls at me.

'Tell me now!'

'It's not safe to talk here.' I lean close. 'I'll tell you later. I promise. But not here.'

She doesn't answer. Just glares.

I lower my voice.

'Do what you did before, OK? Keep me in sight but stay back. And watch for signals.'

She looks down, trembling. She's on the edge, Bigeyes, over the edge maybe. I can't be dealing with this. Not here. It's too dangerous. I got to move and I got to make her move with me.

I check the street, slip out, cut down the pavement, glance behind.

She's following, but she's walking like a dimp. She's got to smack this. There's a speed, a right speed, and she's got to sting it. Not too fast, not too slow. Sometimes you got to run, sometimes you got to creep. But sometimes you got to just take it cool and cute.

She's moving too slow. Shoulders hunched, eyes like stones. Glances over, skims my face. This is bad, Bigeyes. She's like a dead troll looking for a new grave. I got to get her off the street.

I stuff the bag and my old coat into a bin, trig back, check round, take her hand.

'Come on, Bex.'

I walk her on faster. She doesn't pull back, try to let go. Lets me lead her. But her hand's limp in mine. No pressure, nothing. Maybe it's best. She still looks dead to anyone watching but at least she's moving and I can cut off the street just down from here.

By the post office, see? Little side road. Takes us somewhere I can give her a break. Before we crack the next bit. Long as we get to the post office before some neb asks her what's wrong.

On, on.

Almost there. Just a bit further.

Shit, two porkers coming from the left, gobbos.

Bex hasn't clapped 'em. But she's not clapping anything right now. She's got her head down, and she's crying again. Jesus, we're clemmed if they're coming for us.

Bex looks up, catches my eye. She still hasn't seen 'em. I'm watching cute. Checking her, checking them. They might not be hitting us. Hard to tell. But they're heading over. I lean close to Bex, speak soft.

'When I let go your hand, walk on and cut down that side road. By the post office. Got it? Don't look at me. And don't look left. There's two policemen coming over.'

I feel her head start to turn that way. Squeeze her hand tight.

'Don't. Keep looking straight in front.'

Her head stops, turns back.

'Good girl.' I hang on a moment longer. 'OK, I'm letting go now. Just do what I say. Cut down that road and keep walking. There's a little Methodist chapel halfway down. Wait for me in the doorway.'

I let go her hand, cut across the street. Porkers coming on. One's talking into his spinny. Other's checking round.

Flicks a glance at me as I slip past. But I don't feel him stop, or his mate.

Up the pavement, into the sandwich bar, over to the counter, check through the window. Porkers have stopped on the other side of the street. A third porker's joined 'em, a woman.

Bex has disappeared.

8

'YOU ORDERING OR just standing there?' grumbles a voice.

Look back over the counter. Chubby-face gobbo watching me, snappy eyes. Over the street I catch the porkers moving. Heading towards the post office. Sound of a snort. Glance back and see Chubby frosting his brow. I cut in before he does.

'One tuna and mayo, one ham and salad, one cheese and tomato, one egg and cress.'

'Hungry, are you?'

I don't answer. I'm checking the street again. Porkers have disappeared. Can't tell from here if they've scuffed the way Bex has gone. Or should have gone. Cos I wouldn't bet a bean on her going where I told her.

They've all wigged it anyway. Got to shift my stump case there's trouble. Bex can't handle anything right now. If she ever could. Glance back at Chubby.

He's taking his time, dicking the bread, packing the slices, wrapping everything neat with his fat fingers. Nice job but I wish he'd chug up. I got to blast on quick. Check the street again. And now there's new grime.

Two more gobbos, and they're not porkers.

Or muffins.

Don't ask me how I know.

It's kind of a smell. They don't look different from the other suits shaking shadows up and down the street. Smooth, confident, clickety-clean. But they are different. I'm telling you.

'Something to drink with that?' says Chubby.

'Two bottles of mineral water.'

I catch a look. I'm still watching the gobbos but I catch it. Glance back.

'Please,' I say.

He smugs up, like he's just made a point, fetches the bottles, stuffs everything in a bag. I hand him a note, check the street again. One of the gobbos has pulled out a mobile. Other gobbo's checking round.

'There you go,' says Chubby.

He's holding out the bag.

'And your change,' he adds.

I take everything, step towards the door, stop. Two more gobbos have turned up. And I know one of 'em. I've seen him before. He's from the old days. Can't remember his name. But he's one bastard dronk.

Question is: how to get over to Bex without 'em seeing me.

More nebs crowding into the sandwich bar. Street's getting busier. That should help a bit, but I still need these gobbos to move, even if they don't blast out. Right now they're just blobbing there, checking round. I can't shift till they do.

Chubby chimes in again.

'You all right?'

He's halfway through serving some woman but he's peering across.

'Got a problem?' he calls.

Yeah, yeah. He wants me off his stack. I got to move or he'll make something out of this and the gobbos'll clap it. Out of the sandwich bar, down the pavement, checking the other side. The grinks are wandering down towards the post office, all four. They stop, just by the side road down to the Methodist chapel.

I slip behind a parked van, watch cute.

Two of 'em talking into mobiles. Other two flicking round. This is bad, Bigeyes. Bex hasn't got a chance if they cut down that side road. She'll be slumped in the doorway of the chapel and they'll walk right up to her.

Hang on.

They're not heading down the side road. Cos there's the porkers coming up it. Don't know what this means. They haven't got Bex with 'em. And they're not interested in the four grinks. They're walking past 'em.

And now the grinks are splitting.

Edge round to the end of the van, watch 'em go. They're

not sticking together but trigging off down different streets. Porkers stop just down from the post office. Then they split too.

Over the street, stop at the post office, check round.

Crowds still crunching about, but no porkers, no grinks. None I can see anyway. Down the side road, checking doorways. Methodist chapel's further down but she could have stopped anywhere. It's Bex, remember. She doesn't think cute, even when she's not choked in the head.

Nothing in the doorways. Couple of alleyways, little narrow ones, dead ends. She's not in there. On down the side road. Getting a gripey feeling, Bigeyes. I know we haven't hit the chapel yet but I can't throw it off. She's not going to be there. Don't ask me how I know.

What did I tell you? Empty doorway.

Check round. No sign of her. Could have wigged it at the sight of the porkers. Should have done, if she was thinking good. But her head's blown. She could be anywhere. Check round again.

Iron fence either side of the chapel. Poky little cemetery round the back. I slapped a night in there once, huddled against a gravestone. Middle of winter, rough as death. I was nine years old.

Bex won't be in there.

Only way to the cemetery's through the building or over the fence. And she wouldn't have the blitz to climb this thing. Too high, too visible, pointy spikes at the top. She'd never go for the fence if she saw the porkers coming. They'd spot her too easy. She'd blast off down the road.

But I got this feeling, Bigeyes.

So I better cop a glint in case.

Check left, right. Clear for the moment but it won't be for long. There's too many nebs buzzing. Lob the food bag over, up the fence. Got to do this quick, but it's a bastard to climb. How did I get over this when I was nine? Spikes at the top nicking my trousers. Yank 'em free. Down the other side.

Land soft, pick up the bag.

Concrete here but there's grass round the back. Only a tiny cemetery but it's hidden from the road. Good choice if Bex was trying to hide. But she won't be here. She can't be. Don't know why I'm even checking.

End of the building, stop, glance back. Nobody in the road, nobody fixing me from any of the windows opposite. No sounds inside the chapel. Pretty sure it's all locked up. Round the back of the building, into the cemetery.

And there she is, slumped against a gravestone. Same one I used all those years ago. She's crying her head off. I run over, kneel down.

'Bex.'

She doesn't answer.

'Bex, you did good.'

She goes on crying. I lean closer.

'You did real good. Coming here. It's a great place to hide.'

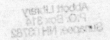

She looks at me, teary eyes.
'But it didn't work, did it?'
She slumps her head again.
'Cos you found me.'

9 I SIT DOWN next to her, lean back against the gravestone. Don't know what to say. She slammed me with that one. Wasn't expecting it. Wasn't expecting to care either. What's going on, Bigeyes?

This caring.

And Bex, of all people.

Caring about Jaz, caring about Mary. That makes sense. But caring about Bex? And what she just said?

She's crying again, head down, like she's forgotten I'm here. I want to do something, make her stop. Can't think of any words that'll do it. And I'm not touching her. She'll bite my hand off. I know it.

I pull out the sandwiches and mineral water.

'I got something to eat, Bex.'

Doesn't even look at it.

'Tuna and mayo.' I hold it out. 'Or we got ham and salad, cheese and tomato, egg and cress.'

She takes no notice. I put the tuna and mayo in her lap. She doesn't touch it, but she doesn't flip it off either. Crying's getting softer. More of a moan now. Head's still slumped on her chest, like she doesn't want to see anything.

See me anyway.

Check round. Big high walls round this part of the cemetery. We're not visible from any angle. She chose good. Probably an accident. But we're cute for the moment. Cold but cute. She stirs suddenly, wipes her eyes with her sleeve, fixes me, looks away again. Takes the sandwich, stares at it.

'Go on, Bex. You got to eat.'

'Piss off.'

She takes a bite, couple more, then flings the sandwich away. It plunks another gravestone, drops on the grass, spills out the tuna. She slumps her head again, but she's not crying now. Except inside. I can feel it. And it hurts. Hurts me, I mean.

Don't know why.

I look down. Can't face her suddenly. She's so full of pain.

And that's when they start.

The flashbacks.

Can't work out why they're hitting now. And yet . . . maybe I do. I'm looking at Bex again and remembering something she said that time she was rowing me ashore from the motor cruiser. About what her father did to her.

Don't suppose she's thinking about that now. She's in

a different kind of pain and it's tied up with Jaz and Dig, and me. But pain's pain and she's unlocked some of mine. I hesitate.

'Do you ever . . . ?'

I stop, look down again. Flashbacks stabbing hard now. Bex is quiet but I'm tensing bad. Got to stop this, got to calm down, front up.

'Ever what?' says Bex.

I take a breath, force out the words.

'Do you ever get memories you can't see, but . . . you still know what happened?'

I look at her now. She's watching me. No expression.

'That home,' I say. 'Where I lived up to the age of four.'

'The one you burnt down.'

'Yeah.'

I bite my lip.

'Those four years . . . they're like a cloud. I can't see anything. Not even the faces. But . . . I know what they did to me.'

I look away. A seagull's flopped down by the tuna sandwich. Nabs at it, flies off. I follow it, arcing over the rooftops. Bex speaks.

'Can't you see none of it?'

'Just the very last bit. Setting fire to the place. I remember that. And getting caught. And bustled off.'

'Where to?'

'Another home.'

'What kind?'

'Tougher.'

'To turn you into a good boy?'

'Yeah.' I stare after the seagull. 'Only it didn't work.'

'You ran away.'

'Lots of times.'

'And they kept catching you.'

'Yeah.'

Seagull's gone. Just rooftops left. And flashbacks. Clear ones now. I reach down, take one of the sandwiches. Hold it out to Bex. She takes it without a word, starts eating.

I pull out another one, take a bite. Egg and cress. Can't hardly taste it. I try and eat but it's no good. Drop the sandwich on the ground.

'I was dead by the time I was four.'

'Eh?' says Bex.

'Dead in my heart. Got moved from place to place. New rules, new punishments. Supposed to make me better. Just made me more angry. Started playing with knives. Found I was good with 'em. By the time I was seven, I was dangerous.'

'So they called you Blade.'

'That was later. When I was ten. Friend of mine started calling me Blade. I was showing off to her. Tricks with a knife. Nothing bad. She wasn't the kind of person you do bad things to.'

'She?'

'Yeah. She.'

I go quiet. I'm not ready to talk about sweet Becky. Specially to her namesake.

Bex doesn't push it. I go on.

'They had other names for me when I was seven. Loads of 'em. I was in trouble everywhere. You name it, I was up for it. Out of control. I was ripe for the picking. So they picked me.'

Silence.

Bex takes a slow breath. I glance at her.

'They catch 'em young, pre-teen. And they know what they're looking for. Kids they can train. Kids who are damaged and want to be part of something. They're the easiest meat. The kids clinging to gangs. The ones who think respect comes from defending your postcode.'

I watch the pictures moving in my head.

'And then there's the others. The kids who don't want to cling to gangs. The loners. The ones who are so badly hurt they don't give a shit. They just want to lash out, hurt back. They're the pick of the lot. Train 'em good and you got a weapon like nothing on earth.'

Bex takes another slow breath.

'That's you,' she says. 'Ain't it?'

I don't answer.

'Ain't it?' she mutters. 'You're a weapon.'

I nod.

'If I was dangerous when I was seven, I was lethal a year later.'

'How lethal?'

'Get caught inside my throwing range and you're dead. If I want you to be. There's nothing I couldn't hit. And hand-to-hand, where it gets creamy—I was even better at that.'

'Really proud of yourself, aren't you?'

'No.'

'You sound like you is.'

She pauses.

'You've killed.'

'Is that a question?'

'Maybe.'

'Well, I don't want to answer it.'

'Think you just did.' Bex frowns. 'So who are these people? The ones what train little kids.'

'Part of a criminal network.'

'What's it do?'

'Same things other criminal networks do. Drugs, trafficking, prostitution, money laundering, protection, usual shit. At the bottom end.'

'The bottom end?'

'Yeah.'

'Meaning what?'

'Meaning that's all I'm telling you right now.'

She studies me, gives a slow scowl.

'So has it got a name? This . . . network?'

I shake my head.

'It's got to have a name,' says Bex.

'Only a handful of people know it exists.'

'But you said it's a network. So there's got to be loads of people in it.'

'There are. Thousands. All over the world. They just don't know they're in it.'

'What?'

'They don't know they're in it. Cos they're being used by the people at the top. And there's only a few of them.'

Bex is watching me cute.

And I know what she's thinking.

She's thinking, if there's only a few nebs at the top who know what's going on, how come I do too? And you're thinking the same thing, aren't you, Bigeyes? Well, think away. Cos it's none of your business how I know.

'You're lying,' says Bex. 'There's no way you could keep a network like that secret. Specially from the people in it. They got to know. Some of 'em anyway. And it's going to leak out. It'll be on the internet somewhere.'

'Well, next time you hit a search engine, type in "criminal organizations" or "secret societies" or whatever. You'll get all the ones everybody's heard of. But you won't find this one. Cos like I say, there's only a few people who know it's there. And they're not telling.'

She runs her eyes over me.

'But you know it's there. So how come you're not telling?'

'Cos it won't make any difference.'

'What do you mean?'

'It won't be enough to bring the bastards down.'

And you know why, Bigeyes? Cos they're too clever. Too well protected. I'm talking about the slimeheads at the top. The spikes further down are more vulnerable and the grinks at the bottom are ten a penny.

But even they're hard to nail.

Cos no one knows who they are. Half the time, they're

brought in from abroad. Come in, do a job, get paid, hike out. Ask no questions. No one to ask anyway. Only neb you deal with is your pay-daddy. All you know is what he tells you. And all he knows is what his pay-daddy tells him.

Lenny and the grunt could have come from anywhere. Probably abroad. Paddy too. And the scumbo in the hospital. As for the wackies we already got here—the pushers, pimps, beefheads, and bruisers—they get used too. Why not cream the home-grown shit when it's sitting on your doorstep?

And it all works the same way.

You only ever see the dreg above you, never the one above him.

Gangs too, they get used, and they're the easiest to shunt. The teens who think they've stepped up, hit the scene, started shifting the big grime. They're not smart enough to see they're just the playthings of other people.

But I shouldn't crow.

Cos that's what happened to me.

Though in a different way.

Another silence. Bex finishes her sandwich. I hand her the last one. She takes it without a word, starts eating. I hold out a bottle of mineral water. She takes that too, sips a bit, looks at me. I guess her question straight off.

'They wanted me cos I was useful,' I say.

She shakes her head.

'They wanted you cos you could kill.'

She frowns.

'You ain't never going to do nothing for Jaz.'

'I want her back as much as you do.'

'Then where is she?'

'I don't know.'

Bex gives a snort.

'That guy in the house said you know where to come.'

'I know where they want me to come. But that's not the place where Jaz is. She could be anywhere.'

'Then we ain't going to get her on our own, are we?' Bex stares at me. 'Might as well call the police.'

'They won't find her either,' I say. 'Not alive anyway.'

Bex turns her head away sharp, like I slapped her. I lean forward.

'But that doesn't mean we can't get her back.'

10

DARKNESS. TOOK ITS time coming. Can't believe I got Bex to wait here this long. She's slept a bit, spite of the cold. Snored even. Funny, grumpy kind of snore.

'Bex.'

She stirs.

'Time to go,' I say.

She yawns, fixes me with her eyes. She's still angry with me. More than that. She still hates me. Don't think she believed a word of what I told her earlier. Maybe you didn't either, Bigeyes.

Well, that's your problem. And hers.

I got enough worries of my own right now. I'm dreading the next thing we got to do. I'm telling you, it's buzzing my brain. First cos of Bex. Got no idea how she's going to react to what I got planned. And second cos of the person we're going to see.

Best-case scenario: we scrape through.

Worst-case scenario: don't even think about it.

Bex is still watching me. There's so much in her eyes now. Anger and hatred—I already told you about them—but there's other stuff too. Sadness, fear, mistrust.

Disappointment.

Yeah, disappointment. In me. I can see it. Like she'd let herself hope for a moment that I might just be able to do something. But she's woken up and the hope's gone. Cos her belief's gone. And now the eyes are spitting at me.

Jaz is dead, they say, and it's your fault.

'We got to go, Bex.'

Stand up, walk to the side of the building. Glance round at Bex. She hasn't even asked where we're going. Doesn't care. Look at her face. See? Doesn't give a shit any more.

'Bex, listen . . .'

'What?'

'You got to have some money.'

I pull out the wodge, hand it to her. She takes it, stares, counts the notes.

'Jesus!' she mutters. 'Five hundred quid?'

'Take it.'

She looks up at me.

'Going to tell me now, are you? Where you got it?'

'Riff's pockets.'

'What?'

'Back at the old house. Remember? When we ran

downstairs and out? I went through Riff's pockets first. Thought he might have left his jacket cos he had to leg it so quick.'

'I didn't see you.'

'I know you didn't.'

She checks me over.

'Got lucky, didn't you?'

'Yeah.'

I'm not telling her about the twelve grand I got in my other pockets. Didn't think Riff would still have it on him. But it was worth checking. And like Bex said, I got lucky.

'How much you got left?' she mutters.

'About the same as you.'

She doesn't believe me. I can tell from her face.

'Come on,' I say. 'We got to find a taxi.'

'A taxi?'

'Yeah.'

'Didn't go too well last time we got one.'

'Should be better now it's dark. But listen. We got to act normal. Like we're together.'

'I ain't bloody snuggling up or nothing.'

'I don't mean that. Just act like we're mates.' I pause. 'Try and forget you hate me.'

'Yeah?'

She leans close, eyes hard.

'And you reckon that's possible?'

I don't answer. She clenches her teeth, grits out the words.

'You killed Jaz. You know that? You killed her. And Dig. And Trixi. They all died cos of you. And Christ knows how many other people there are.' She wipes the spittle from her mouth. 'And you really think it's possible I could ever stop hating you?'

She turns towards the street.

'Let's go.'

'Bex—'

'And don't bother telling me where we're heading. Cos I don't care.'

This is bad, Bigeyes. Worse than I feared. She'll sink us both in this mood. There's that many grinks out watching. I run round in front of her.

She stops, glares.

'Bex, I know you're angry with me—'

'You're frigging right I am.'

'But we still got—'

'Yeah, yeah,' she sneers. 'We still got to be careful. Yeah, yeah.'

'It's dangerous, Bex.'

'Like I give a shit.'

She brushes past me. I run ahead, get between her and the fence.

'Bex.'

She stops again.

'Bex, do you want to just split?'

She stares back at me, raging, hating.

'Do you want to just split?' I say.

She doesn't answer. Just stands there, breathing hard. I

stare back at her, wait. She watches me in silence, then looks away.

'Let's just go,' she mumbles.

I cut to the fence, check up and down the road. Looks cute but I can't see too far from where we are. Got to take a risk. I glance back at Bex.

'I'll go over first. Wait till I give a nod, then climb over. Follow me but stay back, like we're not together.'

'You just said we got to act like we're together.'

'In the taxi, I meant. When we're walking, you stay back. And keep your eyes open.'

Check again. Looks clear.

Over the fence, down the other side. Glance up and down the road. Nod to Bex. She climbs over, quicker than I thought she would. Down the pavement, keeping close to the buildings. Check back.

She's following, about the right distance but she's too close to the road. I nod her towards the shadows. Walk on, cut left, left again, stop.

Got to watch ourselves. We're close to Panky Station and there's always lots of nebs round there. Grinks'll be checking it too so we can't use the taxi rank. We'll cut over the road and hook a cab on the other side.

Check round. Bex is still keeping back, but she'll have to move in again soon. I bung her a look. Doesn't catch it. I try again. This time she nods back. I got to stop her doing that. But not now. She's trigging over.

I wait till she's close, then cross the road. She follows, just a bit apart. Traffic building up. Taxis and smellies mostly. Hit the other side, whip a glance at Bex. She joins me, checks the road.

'There's one,' she says.

I got my hand out already. Taxi pulls over, window slots down. I lean through, give the driver the address. He pulls a face but doesn't say no. I climb in after Bex. She's acting good so far. Not friendly but cute enough. Catch the gobbo's face in the mirror.

He's not happy. And I don't blame him.

Who wants to drive into the Den?

But he sets off. Heading for Mother Grime. I lean forward.

'What you going this way for, mate?'

'Who's driving, me or you?'

'Just wondering.'

'There's road works,' he grumbles. 'So we got to cut down to the river and round.'

'Fair enough.'

I lean back, move closer to Bex. She doesn't pull away. I look at her. She's staring out the window and I can tell she doesn't want to talk. That's cool cos I don't either. Long as she doesn't fizz up again or do something stupid.

Cos she could. Any moment. Check her out.

She's still boiling inside.

I look away, out the window. Feels weird seeing the Beast again. Like nothing's changed in the last three years. Hard to think some nebs like this place. I'll always hate it.

'Sorry about this,' says the driver suddenly.

I check ahead. Couple of cars pranged together and a porker directing the traffic. Driver sniffs.

'Shouldn't be a problem. We'll get round this way.'

He cuts off right. Good choice. I'd have done the same. End of the road, left again and there's Dingdong and the old Toffhouse straight ahead, and Mother Grime flowing past 'em. Left at the bottom and now we're moving fast, river on the right.

I glance at Bex. She's staring out the window at the prickly water. I can't bear to see it, even in the dark. We're shifting now, like the driver wants to get this over with. But I can understand that.

The Den's the Den.

It's not the only bad district—there's plenty more in the Beast—but you wouldn't want to live there. He'll drop us off and wig it. And he won't be looking for a fare back. Cos you don't hang about in that place.

Can't believe this guy. He's hammering the motor. Going to get stopped if he clatters on like this. Check right. Mother Grime still loping past. Spinner bright and clear on the other bank. And there's the Coffin straight ahead.

History's shithole.

Jesus, I hate monuments.

But now it's behind us and we're cutting on east. River's fallen back. Good bloody riddance. But I can't think of that. I got my head full again. I got pictures flooding like before, only now it's all the same one. The face of a woman. Last time I saw her, she said she'd kill me if I come back.

Maybe she will.

Taxi's still cranking too fast. Or maybe it's me. Shit, Bigeyes, it is me. I'm looking at the speedo and it's cute. Driver's spot on the limit. It just felt like he was belting. It's not him moving too fast. It's me. My thoughts.

My fears.

Cos I'm scared that what's coming is coming too quick.

On, on. No monuments here, just dark dives, dark streets. Shadows on corners, shadows in windows, shadows in shadows.

'Left at the end, mate,' I call.

'I know where it is,' comes the answer.

I catch a glance from Bex. Still angry, still bubbling underneath. Looks away again, like she doesn't want to see me. Driver cuts left, jets through the estate. Knows his way round. I'll give him that. Even in the Den.

End of the estate, right towards the shops, left by the old cinema. Pulls over, fixes me. I take no notice. I'm sniping the streets.

Group on the far corner. Five of 'em, teenagers. Three dronks, two trolls. Another group over by the playground. Six dronks. No, seven. No sign of any gobbos.

Driver gives a cough.

I hand him the money, snap the change. We climb out. Taxi screams off. Figures moving either side of the street. Not towards us. Just moving.

As they watch.

Bex edges close.

'I don't like this,' she murmurs.

'It's OK.'

I turn left, away from the figures. They don't follow. Got to walk a bit. Didn't give the driver the real address. I gave him the next street. Just in case. Check back. Still not being followed, just watched. Right at the junction, down the road.

And there's the house.

Same as it always was. Crumbly, tatty, tiles loose. Upstairs window boarded. Cheap curtains downstairs. I can see a shape moving against 'em, a shape I know. They flick apart, close again. And I know she's seen us.

I'm trembling, Bigeyes. And I can't stop myself.

The shape moves again inside the house. I take a breath, walk up to the door, Bex beside me. I don't bother to ring. Sound of footsteps inside, then a pause. A long one.

Door opens, and there she is.

Scowling.

'Hello, Ruby,' I say.

11

SHE LOOKS OLD, Bigeyes, ancient. Can't believe how bad she looks. Can't be more than thirty. Used to be a stinger, spite of working the streets. Smartest black woman out there, the alleybums used to say. Know what they called her?

Black Magic.

Well, check her out now. Is that what three years does to you? Or maybe just the last three years. Cos they won't have been good for her.

She's dressed bad too. Never used to be. Didn't look scrubby ever. Class act, whatever she was doing. Too good for the clapheads who spiked her over. Looks wasted now. Dronky skirt, dronky blouse, half-on, half-off.

But the eyes watching me are the same as ever.

Jesus, Bigeyes. It's hard to know who hates me more.

Ruby or Bex.

'This is Becky,' I say.

Ruby sniffs.

'No, it ain't.'

Same voice. Rich and husky. She flicks an eye at Bex.

'That ain't Becky.'

Turns suddenly, leaving the front door open, sets off up the stairs. I catch a glance from Bex. Step in, up the stairs after Ruby. Hear Bex close the door behind and follow.

Rickety landing. No carpet. Two floorboards missing. Bathroom and bedroom, nothing else, both doors open. Smell of vomit from one, candles from the other.

Ruby's in the bedroom, back to us, facing the boarded window. Walk in, Bex on my shoulder, stop, check round. Chaos of clothes, blankets, empty crisp packets. Single bed, no sheets. Ruby looks round, steps aside.

And something closes round my heart.

Cos there she is.

My little beauty.

My black-skin, fairy-eyed beauty.

'That's Becky,' Ruby says.

The photograph stares back, straight at the camera, straight at me. Like the last time I saw her, three years ago. Could have been taken that day. Both of us just eleven. I find I can't breathe. All this time I've just had memories. And now it's like she's here. I know she's not. It's just a photo on top of a dresser, candles burning either side of her. A little shrine to a memory.

But it feels like she's here. And I want to hold onto that.

Ruby squares up to me.

'That's Becky,' she snarls.

I feel Bex stiffen. Ruby's eye flickers over her, falls on me again.

'Bad idea you come back.'

She pauses, flame-shadows ripping her cheek.

'I don't got nothing no more. No food, no drugs, no drink. Spend all my shit on candles.' She pauses again, watching me. 'But I do got this.'

Opens a drawer, pulls out a gun, points it at me.

'You got sixty seconds to tell me what happened.'

'Jesus!' shouts Bex.

'You can go, girl,' says Ruby. 'It's him and me.'

Fixes me hard.

'And you got fifty seconds now.'

Bex scampers out the room, down the stairs. No sound of the front door but I hear her pacing up and down. I stare back at Ruby.

'I'll talk. But we got to deal first.'

'You're not here to deal! I told you last time—'

'Yeah, you told me you'd kill me.' I take a step closer. 'So why'd I just walk up to your front door?'

'Forty seconds.'

'Must be thirty by now.'

'Piss off!'

She grips the gun with both hands. I take another step closer.

'I'll tell you about Becky. If you look after my friend.'

The pacing stops below. Sound of footsteps creeping

back up the stairs. Ruby's arm wavers, straightens again. Her eyes are hard. But her mouth's trembling.

'Is Becky alive or dead?' she says.

'Help my friend and I'll tell you.'

Footsteps on the landing. They stop outside the room. I can hear Bex breathing as she listens. Ruby sways on her feet. Looks bombed, choked. Could easily shoot me by accident.

'Help my friend,' I say. 'And I'll tell you about Becky.'

Ruby lowers the gun, slumps on the bed. Stares over it.

'We used to sleep in this thing,' she mutters. 'Becky and me. Only bed we got. So we crammed in together. Not much room but we managed. Like we always done. Till you shoved your stinking face in.'

Glares up at the door.

'Who the hell are you?'

Bex is standing there, watching.

'I'm Becky,' she says. 'Honest. It's my name. But some people call me Bex. Blade always does. Don't know why he called me Becky just now.'

Ruby gives a snort.

'Then you ain't worked out what a manipulative little bastard he is.'

'Yeah, I have,' says Bex.

They stare at each other, neither speaking.

Hiss of candles, then silence. Just my heart pounding as I look at the photo again. Sweet Becky. The shadow of a dream. And you know what, Bigeyes? There's something of Jaz in that face.

No question.

Yeah, I know. You're thinking it's just me wanting to see it. And you'd have a point. I mean . . . there shouldn't be anything. Black girl age eleven, white girl age three. But there's something I noticed before. Something I spotted that very first time I saw Jaz's face, when she was hiding under the bed.

She reminded me of a snowdrop.

And that's it. The thing they both got. Cos even though Becky could never look like a snowdrop, she always looked like a little flower. To me anyway. Same as Jaz. Another little flower.

Jesus, Bigeyes.

I hope they're not both dead.

'Is Becky alive?' says Ruby.

I look at her. Mouth's still trembling. Eyes still hard. But she's forcing 'em like that. They're hard cos she's angry. But they're also hard cos she's holding tears down. Taking all her will to do it. Taking all my will to do this too.

Be hard back.

But I got to be hard. Got to force myself. Cos I got to deal.

Or Ruby'll never do what I want.

'I'll tell you,' I answer, 'if you promise to look after Bex.'

But Bex has got her own ideas.

She moves so quick I don't have time to stop her. Jumps over, grabs my hair, shoves me back against the wall, face thrusting close. I catch Ruby staring from behind, confused, scared. Bex doesn't see her. She's fuming too hard at me.

'Tell her,' she breathes. 'Tell her what she wants to know.'

'Keep out of it, Bex.'

'Tell her!'

She whips round, blasts a question at Ruby.

'Kid in the photo, she your daughter?'

'Yeah.'

'And you don't know what's happened to her?'

'No.' Ruby looks down. 'But he does.'

Bex whirls back, eyes flashing. I try to squeeze from her but she crabs me against the wall, hands round my neck.

'Is Becky alive or dead?'

'Bex—'

'Tell her!'

'Bex, listen—'

She lashes out, a full-on punch. Claps me on the cheekbone, smacks my head into the wall. Another punch. I try and block it, miss. Plunges into my chin. And here's her hands tight round my throat, squeezing.

But here's Ruby, too, and she's not after blood.

'Easy, girl, easy. He's not worth it.'

Bex clings on, eyes digging into me. Then suddenly she lets go, turns away, claps a hand to her face. Ruby puts an arm round her shoulder, looks over at me.

'You better go.'

'Ruby—'

'I look after your girl.' Ruby frowns. 'You don't got to do nothing for me. Just go.'

I reach into my pocket, pull out the money I had ready. Ruby glances at it.

'Don't want no money.'

'Five hundred quid.'

'Don't want no money. Not from you.'

'I'll leave it downstairs on my way out.'

Bex has started crying, her face buried in Ruby's shoulder. But she looks up, glowers at me.

'You was always going to dump me.'

I don't answer.

'Like you dumped Jaz,' she goes on. 'Like you dump everybody. Becky too, yeah?'

I shake my head.

'Bex, listen . . . I wanted you to stay with Ruby cos those people . . . the ones after me . . . they never knew I came to this house. Becky was a secret friend. I kept it quiet from everybody. So you should be safe here. And Ruby's got a kind heart. Even though she hates me.'

I feel my words fall like stones. Ruby and Bex just stand there, silent, bonded against me. I look at the photo. Becky's still smiling. Like nothing's wrong. Like nothing ever was.

'Bex?' I say.

She doesn't speak. I look round, fix her.

'I'm going for Jaz, OK? Cos I think she could still be alive. But I got to do it on my own. You can't help me.

You'll just get in the way. So you got to stay here with Ruby. And wait till I get in touch.'

Bex watches me for a moment, then lifts her face, spits. The gob catches my neck, dribbles down. I wipe it off with my sleeve, look at the photo again. Turn to Ruby.

'Becky's dead,' I murmur.

No answer. I bite my lip.

'I'm sorry.'

I wait for her to ask me more. What happened, where the body is, who did it. But she doesn't. She just stares back at me. No tears, no trembling, no shouting. Just a long, unwinking gaze. Then a slow darkening of the eyes, like a shroud's being pulled over 'em.

I turn away, cut down the stairs, stop at the bottom. Drop the money on the mat.

Slip out the door.

12

HOOD UP, DOWN the street, moving fast. Shadows on both pavements, front and behind. Might not be interested in me. Can't tell yet. But I got to be careful with all this jippy on me. And worse still.

The chance of being recognized. There's plenty of nebs'll know me in the Den, even if they haven't seen me for three years. And plenty more who'll know about me from the news.

Wound in my head doesn't help. The newspaper article mentioned the knife slash so that's going round too. I've stopped wearing the bandage and my hair hides the mess pretty good, but the cut's still visible. Bit angry with myself for not sorting it better. I should have fixed something to cover it up.

Still, the Den's a big place and I'm hoping I'm cute round here. I was dead careful when I used to see Becky. Didn't want to plug any grime on her and Ruby, so I kept away from their house as much as possible. Never even went in there before today.

Let's hope none of these nebs have worked out who I am.

'Blade,' mutters a voice.

Shit.

It's coming from over the road.

'That's him,' says the voice.

Not talking to me direct, just gobbing to a mate. But it makes no difference. They've hooked me first go. Flick a glance over. Two dronks, about sixteen, tracking me down the other pavement. Couple of trolls sauntering behind 'em.

Just watching so far. Don't know if they saw me come out of Ruby's place. Jesus, I hope not. This is bad, Bigeyes. Didn't think I'd get skewed in this street. Even with my name banging the news.

Don't recognize any faces.

More figures ahead, lounging by the bus stop. Same sort of age. Glance behind. Shadows following, both pavements. Think it's all teens whipping this street. Three or four talking on mobiles. Keep catching the same word.

'Blade.'

'Blade.'

'Blade.'

It's like a whispery echo. They're not firing it off, just talking low to each other. Hanging back too, so far. I'm sensing they're wary. They know what I can do, or they've heard about it from others, and the gump on the news has linked me with murders, so they're staying safe for the moment.

I got to use this.

Walk on, steady pace. Leave the hood up. They've smacked who I am but I'm keeping my face dark. Gang still lounging by the bus stop ahead. Four dronks, two trolls, all watching. Over to the right, a couple snogging on a bench. They break apart as I draw close, stare at me.

I check the six standing.

They've stiffened, two of the guys fingering their pockets. Both the trolls too. Guy from the bench stands up, his girl still clinging to him. He shakes her off, fixes me. Big dronk, quick eyes, beanie on his head.

'Blade,' he growls.

Not so wary, this crew. Least three of 'em looking to rip. Which case I got a problem. Cos I can't fight 'em, not without a knife. So it's a straight choice. Run or spin their heads. Yeah, right.

We both know I'm a crap runner.

So it's a bum flush. I got to sting one on 'em. If I can.

Fix the big guy. No question he's the beef. Crack him and I crack the others. He's walked out in front of 'em but he's stopped now. I keep walking, walking, walking—stop.

Arm's length from him.

Right hand in my pocket.

I don't move. Not a muscle. Just stare out from under my hood, head back in the folds. He's watching me close, trying to see more of me. This is where it gets skinned, Bigeyes. Next few seconds. I nail him or I don't.

He's looking for someone he can beat in front of his girl. Someone he can smug about, someone with a reputation. He's heard about me and he's thinking— this kid's small. It should be a whack stuffing him over. But he's peering hard just to check I'm not the one thing he's scared of.

A psycho.

And that's what I got to make him see when he looks inside my hood.

It's not about fighting now. It's about will and chill. Dead eyes, dead heart, and letting him see both. I stare up at him, cold, cold, through his face and out the other side.

He's not moving now. He was edging closer, but he's stopped. He's as still as I am. Now's the moment, Bigeyes. If he moves back, I got him. If he stays, I'm hanging.

He stays.

I watch, wait, breathe out the words.

'There's blood all down your body.'

He doesn't speak, doesn't move. I lean close, whisper.

'Cos I just cut your throat.'

I hold his eyes, keep my right hand in my pocket. Reach up with my left, smooth back my hood so he sees the wound. Ease the beanie off his head. Slip it on mine.

Wait.

He stares back, face like stone. I stay still, watching his eyes. Doesn't matter about the rest of him. He's clenching and unclenching his fists—I can feel it—and his body's rippling with tension, but it's all in the face now. He blinks suddenly, takes a step back.

I go on watching. He won't move quick. He's got to save some spit with his crew, and I got to let him. They'll jump me if I play this wrong. But they're splitting already. Big guy's turned and he's stomping over to the other pavement.

Rest of his slugs follow, checking me as they go. None of 'em speaking but they're watching wary. Didn't hear what I said to their dronk cos I talked so low. But they've picked up who won.

So he's still got a problem.

Trouble is—so have I. Cos there's more shadows closing in. Only here's something else. A smelly. Number 24. Oh, you beauty. Doesn't cruise the way I want to go but who gives two bells? It'll get me out of here.

Pulls over at the stop, doors open.

Nobody gets off. I check round. No dregs belting in but they're all watching. Climb on, pay the driver, sit down, front seat, back to the other passengers, hood up again, over the beanie. Doors close. Bus grunts off down the street.

I keep my eyes in front. Don't need to check behind. I clapped the other passengers when I got on. All muffins. Driver's no gripe either. Hardly looked at me. Probably guffed to his brain picking up teenage slugs. The Den's crackling with 'em so I guess another one makes no difference to him.

I'm thinking hard. I've paid for five stops but I might get off sooner and change buses. Point is, Bigeyes, I know where I got to go, but I got lots of nebs to avoid. Maybe smellies are the best way to get about this time of the evening. Long as I keep my head down and watch cute.

Street's behind us now and we're turning right. Past the park, past the old school, through the shopping centre. None of this has changed, Bigeyes. It's like I just left yesterday. Almost expect to see Becky standing outside the Half Moon Café.

Over there on the left. Got it?

Dronky pit but we used to meet there after she finished school. I never went. To school, I mean. Not ever. But Becky did. Used to like it, she said. She had this little satchel and she'd wait for me outside the Half Moon, and we'd go in and have milk shakes and sticky buns, and she'd pull out all her exercise books, and show me what she was doing.

I wasn't that interested. I just loved being with her, listening to her talk, hearing her laugh. She had this kind of gurgle. She'd find something funny and start chuckling, and then she couldn't stop. It used to make her whole face light up. Yeah, I loved being with her.

But then Ruby found out she was meeting me on the way home from school. Becky hadn't told her. And Ruby said she had to stop, cos I was bad shit. Which was true. So I thought up other ways me and Becky could meet. Secret ways Ruby didn't know about.

And that's when everything went wrong.

But I can't think about that now. Cos I got a new problem. Smelly's pulling over at the next stop, there's two gobbos waiting to get on, and I recognize 'em.

Grinks.

13 SEEN 'EM BEFORE, both gobbos. I know which spike they work for. And what they can do. Tell you something else, Bigeyes. They're not here for a ride.

Grinks drive. They crack about in cars. They don't jump on tube trains or buses. Only time they hit the snakehole or hook a smelly is when they're looking for someone.

I got to get off. And I got to time it right. Won't be easy cos I'm the gig.

The reason they're here.

So they'll be watching cute.

Out of the seat, hood still up, beanie low. Slip down the bus to the middle door. Faces flip up at me as I pass. No problem with 'em so far. Couple of old dunnies. Boy with his mum and dad. Gobbo listening on headphones.

No one's taking much notice.

Check round. Moment the grinks get on, I got to get

off. Won't work if they've seen me from the road. Or if they already know I'm on the smelly. They won't get on at all. One'll be waiting by the middle door, other at the front.

Bus stops.

Doors open.

I duck my head, keep as low as I can. Glance round. Nobody's waiting outside the middle door. But no one's got on at the front either. Driver calls out suddenly.

'You getting on or what?'

I flick a glance at him. He's shouting into the street. Sound of a mutter, both gobbos. They're not answering the driver. They're mumbling to each other. I see the driver turn.

Catch his eye. He's getting angry. First he's got two gobbos hanging about in the street, now he's got the kid with a beanie blobbed by the middle door. And no one's moving. In a moment he's going to bawl back at me. Ask me if I'm getting off or staying.

And the grinks'll pick up I'm here.

Then I see it. The first of the grinks getting on.

Just the top of the guy's head.

I duck further, edge out the middle door, foot on the street. Check round the side of the bus. Shit, the second grink's still standing outside. Hasn't even started to get on. I need him to follow his mate or I'm plugged.

He sniffs, flicks his head, a little backward tilt. I've seen him do that before, Bigeyes. It's a mannerism. Makes him feel important, like he's sneering down on everybody.

Don't ask me how I know.

Hasn't looked my way yet. But he could any moment.

Come on, you bastard. Get on the smelly.

Shadow appears, top right corner of my eye. First grink's moving towards the middle of the bus. Couple more seconds and he'll see me standing here, one foot on, one foot off.

But I still can't move till Flickyhead gets on. Shadow moves closer. I got to go, got to risk it. Even if the other grink stays put. Off the smelly, down towards the back, low as I can. I'm waiting for the shout, the thump of footsteps.

Nothing.

Just the sound of the doors closing, the bus pulling away.

Creep to the side of the road, slip behind a parked car, check round. Smelly's rumbling off down the street. Can't see either grink. Wait, check round. Got to make sure they didn't both get off. But there's no sign of 'em.

Straighten up, breathe hard. I'm knotted up, Bigeyes.

And I'm still stuck in the Den.

Right, change of plan. Forget about using smellies. Dimpy idea. The grinks are obviously checking everything. Can't use the snakehole either. Taxi maybe, if I see one and it looks safe. But I don't suppose there'll be many in the Den right now. Nobody goes snacking for a fare in this trough, specially after dark.

OK, I know what I got to do. And we better shift, Bigeyes, cos time's ticking. So stay close and keep your spark fresh. We got to see everything.

Over to the other pavement, down the path, left at the church, over the square, past the bank. Check round, all the time. Plenty of nebs to keep an eye on. Muffins so far, even the teens in doorways, but we got to watch.

Every second.

I'm keeping the hood up and the beanie pulled low. That dronk turned out to be useful. Beanie hides the wound and it's warm too. Least I don't stand out too bad here. Lots of other kids punching the streets and most of 'em look like me in the darkness.

But I still got to be careful. Got recognized down Ruby's way, so anything can happen.

Shadow moves down to the left. Might not be anything. Walk on, steady pace. Shadow shuffles, falls still. It's a duff, sitting there. Shaven-head guy. Can't be more than eighteen. Stares up at me, face like a grave.

Maybe that'll be me one day.

Eh, Bigeyes? Four more years and I'll look like him.

If I live that long.

Closer, closer. He's still watching me. I wait for him to call out. He's going to ask for some jippy. And I can't give him any. Not cos I don't want to. I just can't stop. It's too risky.

But he doesn't call out. Just watches. I walk past, on, on. Stop, turn, go back. Flick him a coin. It falls in his lap. He looks down at it, back at me, says nothing. I walk on. End of the street, left, down to the bottom, and there it is, over the road.

The Prince William.

Got to be the ugliest pub in the Den. And that's saying something, Bigeyes. But I'll tell you what. It's got one big advantage. Lots of nebs use it and most of 'em aren't too brained up.

Check it out.

Lights on, clunky music, sound of laughter. Check the traffic. Smelly rolls past, motor bike, another smelly. Empty road. Except for something sticking over the edge of the kerb.

Something round.

Walk over.

It's an old football. Pick it up, squeeze it. Lost a bit of air. Dronky thing. Some kid probably flipped it on purpose. Check round. Cars moving down from the top end, couple more the other way. Turn my face, let 'em pass, turn back.

Give the ball a bounce, catch it.

Trig over the street.

Prince Willy's getting noisy. Some gobbo's started up a song. Round the back, into the car park. Lots of motors there already. Bounce the ball again. Hold it still. Slip into the shadows, crouch.

Wait.

14 WON'T STAY QUIET for long. Not Prince
Willy. Here we go.

Car pulling in.

Slip off my coat, push it out of sight. Not the place
for a hood. I got to look like some kid who's just nipped
out of his house. But I'll keep the beanie on. Grip the
football, watch. Cute motor, stops, other end of the car
park.

Four dolls.

They get out, laughing, head towards the pub.

No good. Let 'em go. Never mind why, Bigeyes. I know
what I'm looking for and they're not it. More cars, two of
'em. No, three. Now it's looking promising.

Young gobbos. Three in the first car, four in the second,
two in the third. They spill out, slam the doors. One of
'em sees the dolls hitting the pub porch, calls out.

'Hey, girls! No rush!'

Other gobbos leer and strut. Dolls take no notice, disappear inside the pub. All the gobbos out now, cocking their stumps round the car park. Easy piss, Bigeyes. You got no idea what a whack this is. I've checked 'em all out. Any one'll do.

I step out, bounce the ball, bounce it again.

'Hey, kid!'

One of 'em's sticking me with his eyes.

I bounce the ball again. They all fix me. And now it's playtime. They're bollocking their heads off, shouting for the ball.

'On me head, boy!'

'Here, mate!'

'C'mon! C'mon!'

I walk in among 'em. Chuck the ball up. They're like flies on jam. Couldn't be easier. They don't give me back the ball, but that's cute. I don't want it. They kick it, head it, lose interest, hack it off into the road, slack over to the pub, hooting.

I wait till they've disappeared, pull out the car keys. Couldn't make up my mind which motor I want. So I creamed two lots of keys. One from the gobbo with the best car. Other from the guy who pissed me off most.

No contest really.

Got to leave the flash one. I'd love to poke it about but it's too risky. Every neb on the street's going to turn and cop a glint at that one. I'll take the other motor. More of a dingo so it's safer. And like I say, the guy pissed me off. Sniggered at me as he booted the ball away.

Back to the side of the car park, pick up the coat, put it on. Over to the flash car, check the pub again. All clear. Leave the keys on the bonnet. Some other dronk might want a free ride. No, hang on. Guy wasn't that big a dung-pot. He can keep his motor.

Stick the keys on the front wheel.

Over to the dingo. Unlock it, get in, eyeshine over the tricky. All cute. Key in the ignition, turn. Engine fires. Check the petrol gauge. Off we go.

Out of the car park, left down the road, up to the top, left at the lights, on to the roundabout. Christ, Bigeyes, feels so weird driving round this patch again. I used to jack motors round here for the hell of it.

Past the playing fields, down to the railway station. First time I saw Becky was outside here. She was with a mate but she smiled at me. I'll never forget it. Didn't say anything. Just smiled. Same smile like she had in the photo.

But that first one was special. Whipped me up big time. Made me feel so happy I had to buzz round the corner and smash a window. That old warehouse, see it? Window's round the back. They probably still haven't fixed it.

That's what Becky did to me. Just by smiling. Made me feel like I was worth something. And it was even better when she talked to me. First person to do that. Proper talking, I mean. That's why I loved her. First person to talk to me. First person to care.

Maybe the last one too.

Only . . . no.

She's not the last. I know that. Cos things have changed.

I never would have expected it. But Mary cares about me too. Don't ask me why. I was spitty with her in the beginning. Didn't trust her at all. But I do now. And I know she cares.

If she's still alive.

Got to stop thinking like this. It's blamming my brain. And I got to slow down too. I'm driving too fast and you know why? It's cos I'm shook up over Becky and Mary. And now I got Jaz in my head. Like she's ever anywhere else.

And she's shaking me up too.

Slow down, dimp. Slow bloody down.

Got to drive legal, Bigeyes. There's that many nebs looking for me now. Porkers to the right, see? Too late. You missed 'em. Look better next time. There were two of 'em, women.

Left, down to the bottom, onto the main road. We're heading west, case you're wondering, but we won't be for long. Just a bit further towards the centre, then we cut right and slam the north-east.

Cos there's a place I got to go.

Before I sort out the big stuff.

Got a busy night ahead of us, Bigeyes. And before it all starts, there's something else I got to do. Off the main road, down to the right, round the parade of shops. There used to be a takeaway here. Little kebab shop. Smelly place but quiet.

There it is.

Only now it's pizzas.

Who cares? Pull over, glance round. Feels cute but I got to watch good. There's no part of the Beast that's not dangerous. Check pockets, shift some of the jippy. Stuff a few notes round my dingers.

Out of the car, into the takeaway.

Back again, safety belt, lock the doors. Bolt down the pizza, sink the Coke. Start up, back to the main road, up onto the flyover. Right, Bigeyes, look ahead. Go on, straight ahead.

Check him out.

The Beast.

One big bastard, isn't he? Even in the darkness you can't miss the size of him. Check out all those lights. And you know what? You're only seeing a tiny bit of him. Like his little toe. He's a giant, Bigeyes, an effing giant.

And he's got more ways to kill than you could ever know.

Yeah, yeah. You're thinking here he goes again. Banging on about the Beast. You're thinking, for Christ's sake, it's just another big capital city. Got its scum, got its dark side, like any other capital city, but most of the nebs are OK.

And maybe you're right. Maybe most of the nebs are OK.

Trouble is, I've never met 'em.

I've only ever met the others.

Down the other side of the flyover, on towards the centre. Least we've left the Den behind. That's a good feeling. Just wish it was going to last. Cos now we're turning right and heading for the Grinder.

That's what I call it anyway.

Different kind of area. Not so beaten up as the Den. Bit more jippy in some of the streets and not so many gangs. But there's bad shit there, mostly spinning drugs, and plenty of hard dronks who'll know who I am.

So I'm not stopping long.

It's blast in, blast out.

Past the brewery, past the school, past the start of the motorway, over the roundabout, right at the lights. Feels good to be heading away from the centre. But I'm doing it again, Bigeyes. Driving too fast.

Slow down, slow down.

Porkers heading the other way. They flash past. Check the mirror. They've gone but now there's another police car, and it's coming up behind. Squeeze the wheel. Check the mirror again.

They might not suspect anything. Might just be driving this way. But I was belting it a moment ago. No question, I was way over the speed limit. Jesus, Bigeyes, if I get plugged cos of something so stupid, something I did myself, I'll never . . .

They're pulling out.

Eyes in front. Keep the speed steady. I can feel 'em, Bigeyes. They're drawing level. Don't look at 'em. Keep driving, keep driving, nice and legal. They're hovering now, just sitting there, edge of my blind spot. I can feel 'em checking me.

Maybe the gobbo who owns the car has reported it missing and the porkers are on it already. Or maybe they're just thinking this kid looks too young to have a driving licence.

They're edging past. This is the moment. If they flash me to the side of the road, I'll pull in and wig it over the barrier. I might just get away. But they're not stopping. Thank Christ. They're driving on.

I slow down, breathe hard, let 'em disappear ahead.

Take the next exit.

And we're in the Grinder.

15 TOLD YOU IT was different, Bigeyes. Check out the houses. Smarter, see? Better cars too. Like I say, more jippy round here than in the Den. But remember the other thing I told you. There's hard nebs here too.

Trust me.

So keep watching.

Cut right, round the edge of the estate. Good news is we don't have to go too far into the Grinder. I chose a cute spot when I cooked this one. You probably think you know what's going to happen next, right?

So I'll tell you something straight up, Bigeyes.

You're wrong.

Don't look at me like that. I can read your chirpy little brain. It's going, 'I remember the bridge over the stream. I remember the overflow graveyard. He's got some diamonds stashed away. Or some money. Or both.'

Well, stuff your brain. Cos it's wrong.

Half-wrong anyway.

Let's get this over with.

Other side of the estate, right at the junction, down the lane, on towards the railway line. Over the bridge, slow down, check round, pull over. Lights off, cut the engine.

Darkness.

Heart's pounding, eyes skudding about. Calm down, calm down. Wait, wait, wait. Open the door, ease out, listen. Close the door, listen again. Yeah, Bigeyes, take it in.

Sounds and silence. Both together.

The sounds of cars rumbling round the Grinder, the traffic further off. The sounds of the Beast. The deep heavy breaths as he rolls and roars.

And then the silence.

The silence of where I am, standing here by the railway line. Like I'm in a little glass bulb. My silence. Just my thoughts whispering inside me.

Check round.

No shadows moving. None I can see anyway. Think the railway line's deserted. Hope so anyway. You sometimes get duffs slapping it round here. They find a spot among the bushes either side of the railway fence. Don't ask me why.

Dronky place to sleep. Must get woken every time a train rattles by.

Still, I think we're on our own for the moment.

Come on.

Over the fence, down to the tracks, listen again. No

tinkling in the rails, but we got to be careful, Bigeyes. I nearly got slammed here once. Never heard a thing in the rails and suddenly there's a train lomping down.

Just got out of the way in time.

Check the tracks, both ways.

Dark all round. And quiet suddenly, dead quiet. Not just my silence now. It's like the other sounds have faded. But they're still there, Bigeyes. You can hear 'em if you listen. See what I mean?

And that's what's weird. Cos before, you heard 'em automatic. Didn't have to try. But now we're down here, it's like they've faded. Only they haven't. They've never gone away. It's like you've gone away instead.

Freaks me out a bit.

OK, cut right. Yeah, you guessed it. We're heading under the bridge. Only it's not like with that little stream we went to. We're not going to rip a stone out of the wall. Watch close and you'll see.

Under the bridge, slow, slow. Could still trig into some duff we haven't seen. Or a druggie. Or some couple whamming. Looks cute though. On, on, under the bridge. That's right, Bigeyes. We're going all the way through and out again.

You're wondering why we didn't come down the other bank.

I'll show you.

Out the other side. Now then. Check right and left, top of the banks. See how high the fences are? Much higher than the one we climbed over. I'm telling you, the fences up there are a bogload of trouble to get over. Bank's steeper too.

So it's best to whip over where we did and cut under the bridge.

Anyway, we're nearly there. Up the bank, feeling with my hands. I can see the spot from here, Bigeyes, even in the darkness. Right by the side of the bridge, bushes clustered round, just down from the top.

Check out the fence. We're closer now. See what I mean? No one's going to try climbing that. Duffs and other nebs'll do what's easiest. Hit the other side of the bridge and stay there. They won't bother crabbing round here. Too much fuss.

Which makes this the perfect place.

Cos look.

Push through the bushes, scrabble under the roots and twigs and twisty branches, pull off the bits of broken rock. And there it is.

The old drain.

Just like I left it three years ago.

No water flowing through it now. Been blocked up for God knows how long and forgotten. By everyone except me. Cos it's not empty, Bigeyes, as you probably guessed. But like I said, we're not talking diamonds or jippy here.

Pull off the top, reach in, poke about.

And there's the familiar feel.

And the familiar feeling.

Don't know how to describe it, Bigeyes. Cos it's changed. Since Mary, Jaz, and all the stuff that's happened. It's different now. Used to be a kick, a buzz, a burst of something. Mixture of power and fear.

Now it's just the fear.

But it's still familiar.

And I got something else too. Something I didn't have before.

A reason.

Never had a reason before. Not a right one anyway. So you better listen to this, Bigeyes. Look me in the face and listen good. Remember what I said to you? About tomorrow? I said keep your distance. Cos you won't like what I got to do.

Well, I won't like it either. But it's the only way.

Look down at the drain. Take a breath, pull 'em out.

Both knives.

Check 'em good, Bigeyes. Get used to 'em. Cos this is serious now.

Serious knives for serious work.

No flickies. These are heavy shit.

Go on. Look at 'em. Make yourself do it. And you might as well know. Both of 'em got a history. So here's the thing, Bigeyes. I'm being straight with you. So you know what's what.

Stay with me tomorrow if you want.

But if it bloods up, don't try and hold me back.

Or I'll turn these bastards on you.

OK, enough said. Hook the knives in my belt, pull the coat over 'em. Scramble down the bank, under the bridge, up to the fence, climb over.

Stop.

Listen again.

Gone quiet everywhere. Hear it? Silence all round. And now it's real silence. No traffic, no distant hum, nothing. But we're not the only ones listening.

He's listening too, Bigeyes.

The Beast.

Listening for me. My movements, my thoughts. And now I can hear him whispering, far off. Not here. It's still quiet in the Grinder. But far off, in his soul, he's calling me. And all his stinking minions.

Reach inside my coat, feel the knives.

Feel the feeling.

Whisper back.

'I'm coming.'

16

DRIVE, DRIVE, OUT of the Grinder, into the night.

Sounds have started again. Sound of the engine, sound of other motors, shouts from the streets. Cos there's nebs out, young nebs mostly, cruising clubs, hitting pubs.

And still the Beast goes on whispering in my ear.

Calling, calling.

He doesn't need to. Cos I'm already heading back. But he goes on calling, like he's scared I might bottle out. But I won't. I'm choked up bad, but I'm in. I got the gig clear in my mind.

The Grinder's slipped away and I'm cutting for the centre. Cars hugging close, splash of lights all around. Drink him in, Bigeyes. The Beast's got a different face at night. Like the old city had. Difference is, she could be cute.

He can't.

He's got too much power. It's kind of an energy and it scares me. Cos it's out of control.

Got the old thoughts flooding now.

Becky, Mary, little Jaz.

And Bex. Even Bex.

Can't believe I'm worried about her, but I am. Don't suppose she's worried about me. Maybe she's phoned the police by now. Ruby's probably made her. I might not even get to the place I'm aiming for cos the porkers'll bang me up first.

We've passed three police cars on this road already.

Yeah, I know. You didn't see 'em.

Least one of us is awake.

Off the main road. I want to take some back streets. Got to play it cute to hit the spot I want. Right at the traffic lights, round the park, left at the junction. More shouts. Young nebs again, swilling from bottles.

Drive round 'em, checking good. I know the streets I want. Just a question of getting to 'em. Left, left again, on, on. And here's more young nebs. Blocking the way this time.

Black kids, gathered round something.

Think there's a fight going on. Yeah, I got it. Two trolls rolling on the ground, slamming each other. I can just see 'em. Can't get hooked into this. Check behind. No one pegging my bum. Reverse gear.

Thump!

Something crashes into the front of the car. Check

round. Small rock rolling on the bonnet. Black kid further off, leering at me. Must have seen me, broken apart from the group and flung the rock.

He gives me the finger, turns back to watch the fight.

Squeal the car back, wheel round, race on. Rock bumps off onto the street. Right at the junction. OK, Bigeyes, we're getting close. Keep your eyes open for porkers and grinks. And anything that looks dangerous.

Cos I got to tell you. It's getting hard now.

And tomorrow's going to be a tough shoot.

I got a plan, yeah, but success-wise we're talking fifty fifty.

At best.

There's a hundred things got to go right for this to work. And a hundred things could go wrong, easy. Most of 'em stuff I can't predict. It's hit and hope, Bigeyes.

And I'm scared.

Fifty fifty?

I was lying, talking it up. Truth is, that's a dream. We got nothing like fifty fifty. The odds are so bad I don't want to think about 'em.

But there is one good thing. I got the car sorted. I needed one for the plan but hadn't intended to jack a motor till later. Only problem is the porkers'll be looking for this one already.

And here's another problem.

Traffic lights on red and two porkers standing on the pavement.

Stop the car, check round. They're not looking my way.

Too busy talking to each other. Just hope the lights turn green soon. Here they go.

Shit.

Car in front's stalled. Someone behind me blares a horn. Both porkers swivel round, check over the line of motors. Driver in front starts his car, stalls again. Tries a third time, revs up, moves off. But now the lights are changing back.

I'm not waiting.

Clutch up and go.

Both porkers fix me. I turn my head away, speed up. Halfway over the junction and now there's cars coming right and left, horns yamming. I drive on and over, and now I'm bouncing down the next street. Check the mirror.

Porkers staring after me.

One of 'em talking into his spinny.

Might not mean trouble. There's enough nebs who crash lights and they were only just changing when I went. Big problem is if the porkers check the registration number. They'll pick up it's a nicked car.

On, on. Right at the end, right again.

Got to crank up, Bigeyes, shift our stumps and put some distance between us and the police. Down the street, right at the end, and now watch good. We're cutting left, down this narrow lane.

Quiet little place.

High buildings either side. Check 'em out, Bigeyes. They're offices. Tired old offices. I know cos I've slept in a few of 'em. Easy to break into and most have got attics or storerooms for a doss. But we're not going there.

We're going here.

An even quieter place.

End of the lane, turn left, pull over.

Cut the engine.

How about that? Little cul de sac. And nobody in it. Warehouses on the left, garages on the right. Twelve in a row. Don't need to count 'em. I know there's twelve cos I've been here before. Lots of times.

Out of the car, close the door, check round.

Great spot this, Bigeyes, for all kinds of reasons. First up, we can't be seen. No problem with the warehouses. You're looking at the back of 'em. The nebs who work there are all on the other side. Nobody here anyway this time of night, and it won't be a problem tomorrow, unless we're very unlucky.

Other good thing is the garages.

There's always two or three empty. And even the ones that aren't don't get used much. Look at 'em. They're tatty as hell. I hardly ever saw anyone come here. And they're a whack to break into. Unless someone's dinked 'em up a bit.

But I don't think so. They look even more dronky than they did three years ago. And we only need one. Let's go. First garage.

Door's locked. Check the mechanism. No problem stinging that if I have to but we'll grub out the other garages first. There you go. What did I tell you? Second garage and we're jigging.

Door closes but the lock's broken, see? Open up, check round. Beautiful. Nothing in here but rusty tools and old paint pots. And almost no chance of the owner turning up.

First, he's not using it for his car. If he was, he wouldn't have the tools and pots all over the floor. They'd be pushed to the side or the back. And second, I'm pretty sure he's not using the place for anything else.

Nothing in here except this junk. And look at it. The tools are old and crappy. Haven't been used for ages. And the paint pots are empty. No point looking any further. This'll do.

All I need is a place where I won't be disturbed. And I don't need it for long. Cos in less than a day, this thing'll be sorted, one way or the other. Reach down, shunt the tools and cans to the side. Straighten up, check round.

OK, Bigeyes.

I've found what I want.

17   DRIVE IN, ENGINE off, out of the car, pull down the garage door. Darkness closes around me. I stand there, breathing hard.

Distant sound of traffic. Only it's not so distant. There's cars and smellies and taxis only a short way off. They just sound distant, feel distant, and in the darkness they seem like they're from another world.

Look round, wait for my eyes to adjust. Takes a while, but I'm starting to see now. First time I've noticed there's a shelf on the far wall. Nothing on it but an old oil can.

Feel my breathing slow down.

I'm still standing, Bigeyes. Why'm I doing that? I got to rest, sleep, get ready for tomorrow. But I'm just . . . standing here, staring into the dark. What's wrong with me?

Edge round the car, slip into the driver's seat, close the door. Lock it. Don't know why I did that. Won't make any difference if they get inside the garage. Anyway . . .

Lean the seat back, far as it'll go. Take another breath. Close my eyes. Got to rest, Bigeyes. Got to sleep. Only I can't. All I see is more darkness. Inside my eyes, inside my head. And all the usual faces.

Becky, Mary, Jaz.

And now Bex and Ruby.

I'm so scared about tomorrow. Scared of what'll happen if it goes wrong. And scared of something else too. Myself. Yeah, I'm scared of myself. Open my eyes again.

Darkness is still there. Like it's never going to go away.

There's something I meant to tell you, Bigeyes. I lied to Bex. When I was talking about the network. She asked me if it's got a name, remember? And I said no. And that's true, sort of. Cos like I said, the grinks who get paid to sling the sludge don't get told much. They just carry out orders.

Right now they've been told to find a kid called Blade. When they've sorted him, they'll move on to the next job. And the spikes above 'em do the same. Carry out orders, move on.

None of 'em thinks about a name.

But there is a name, Bigeyes. A private name the slime-heads at the top use when they're talking about the operation. You know what they call it?

The Game.

That's right, Bigeyes.

The Game.

Cos to them, that's what this is. A huge, great game with massive stakes. We're talking power, politics, money, global change. That's what the grinks don't know, or the spikes. They just think they're cracking the usual criminal shit. They don't realize that the stuff they're doing is to finance something bigger.

Much bigger.

Cos the slimeheads are aiming high. I'm telling you, Bigeyes. The Game isn't about fun. Not to them. To them it's about life and death. The Game is all that matters. The Game is to be won. And they're very serious about winning it.

Yeah, yeah. You're wondering how I know.

Well, maybe one day I might just tell you.

But I got to get through tomorrow first.

I just wish I could sleep.

Jesus, Bigeyes, I'm so whipped up inside. I want to dash out, find a phone, ring The Crown, see if Mary's still alive, talk to her. And if she's not, ring Ruby. I know the number. I could talk to her. Or Bex, or . . .

Someone.

I just . . .

Want to talk.

And just for once . . . not be on my own when I'm feeling scared.

Sit up, fix the driver's seat upright, reach under my coat. Pull out the knives. Hold 'em in front of me, blades up.

Didn't think I'd see these bastards again. Didn't want to either. Thought I could leave 'em behind, leave all knives behind. But it doesn't work that way, does it, Bigeyes? Not for me. Even when I throw 'em away, they come back.

But maybe I'm just zipping myself over.

I buried these two, didn't I? Didn't drop 'em in the water like I did that last one. I left 'em to be found again. And I chose to come looking. Maybe some part of me knew I was always coming back to the Beast. To face what I didn't finish when I ran away.

Picture of Jaz floats in front of me.

I swear I can see her. Her little face, staring at me, like it's hanging suspended inside the windscreen. Not smiling or anything. Just staring out, straight at me.

'I love you, baby,' I murmur.

She goes on staring. I whisper to her.

'I never finished that story. But I will, sweetheart. If you're still . . .'

I can't say it. Can't think it. I squeeze the two knives. And for a moment it looks like they're pointing straight at Jaz's head. One each side. I drop my hands quick, stare back at Jaz's face.

But she's gone.

All I can see is the windscreen. I feel tears start inside me. I give a shudder, hold 'em in. I said I wouldn't cry. And I won't. Squeeze the knives tighter, climb out of the car, stand there. I don't know what to do, Bigeyes, and I can feel darkness closing round again.

Inside of the garage is fading.

Everything's fading.

I lean against the wall, slump down it to the floor, rest my head back against the brick. It smells of mould and I can feel a wisp of cobweb. Close my eyes again. And somehow I sleep.

Till a car horn wakes me.

I stiffen, sit up. I'm shaking and it takes me a moment to remember where I am. I feel drugged, cold, and I'm still frightened. Heart's pounding bad. Cos I can see through the gap at the bottom of the garage door. And it's morning. It's time to move.

Scramble up, stretch, breathe.

Think.

Keep to the plan, keep to the plan.

But get ready to change it. Cos anything can happen when the spit starts to fly.

I'm still holding the knives, Bigeyes, one in each hand. Put 'em away, out of sight. They're ready. And so am I. Just one more thing to find. Bound to be something I can use in this garage. Check among the old tools.

This'll do.

Small hammer. Light but strong. Hope I don't need it but best to have it in case. Stuff it in a pocket. Coat's bulging now, what with all the jippy as well. But I can't help that. I'm not leaving the money behind.

And I won't care about it anyway, if today goes bad.

Over to the garage door, listen. No sounds outside, apart from the early traffic humming round the Beast.

Ease the door open, check out. Hard to tell what time it is. I'm guessing half six. Back to the car, check the clock.

Shit, it's ten past seven.

We got to shift.

18 WE'RE MUCH LATER than I meant to be. And there's stuff to do before I hit the gig. Jump in the car, turn the key. Engine fires. Reverse out, close the garage door, back in the car.

Down the lane towards the main road.

OK, Bigeyes, we're going somewhere you've been before. When we get to the end of the road, check right. Hold on, wait. OK, look now.

Recognize that road?

Jesus, you don't, do you? Never mind.

Down the road, slow, steady. Got to stay legal, look normal. Lots of cars about already so we don't stand out too bad, but the porkers'll be looking for this motor. I only need it a bit longer so I'm hoping we'll be cute, but we still got to be careful.

OK, now look.

Left side of the road. See? That's where we hooked the

taxi. And the grinks nearly closed us in. There's the allotment we ran through. That's right, Bigeyes.

We're coming back to the first place I showed you.

The very first.

Up to the roundabout, second exit. Check right. See the turning? The little street? Me and Bex ran down that when the grinks found us in the alleyway. And guess what. We're cutting down it again.

Right now.

You're thinking this is crazy, heading back to where they found us before. But I'll tell you something. It's no riskier than anywhere else in the Beast. And hopefully the grinks won't be expecting us here.

Down the street.

Recognize any of this? Bike sheds? Bank? Don't know why I bother asking. On, slow now, checking round. Pull over. OK, look left. Even you got to remember that.

Shoe shop. Little courtyard behind it. And behind that, the wall me and Bex climbed over from the alleyway. Don't panic. We're not climbing over it again. But we are getting out of the car. Cos I got to go to work. And I'm busted for time cos I slept too long. So we won't slap about.

Out of the car, check the street. Plenty of nebs already, as I expected. Pretty sure they're all muffins, but we got to watch cute. Hood back, beanie down. Walk slow, casual, side of the street.

Got to blend, OK? Stay out of sight. Used to be good at this. Still am but I've lost a bit of confidence. And I'm so choked up with nerves right now I'm worried I might crash up. If there's grinks anywhere near, they'll smell that.

Walk on, end of the street, check round. Turn right, right again.

OK, Bigeyes, check the road in front of you. Go on. Now tell me you don't remember it. You got to. Alleyway down on the right, see? Where me and Bex hid. And over the road, the car park where the home used to be.

The one I burnt down.

Take a breath.

Walk to the jewellery shop, check through the window. Clocks all say different times but the one on the wall says half seven. Got to be right. Which case, I got to buzz on. Check round.

Loads of nebs on the street. Should be spoilt for choice. All I need's a mobile. I'd rather have two or three but I'll settle for one if I have to. Down the street, keeping back.

Woman climbing out of a car. Should be a whack. But I miss her. Old dunny slipping hers into her handbag. I miss that too. What's wrong with me? These are easy slams. But I can't crack 'em. I'm getting so choked I'm freezing up.

Two businessmen, trigging together. Neither holding mobiles. They're just naffing. I got to take a risk. Walk on, heading between 'em, face down like I'm not watching. Feel 'em break apart, step round me.

Walk on, wait, check behind. They haven't stopped.

Slope over to the side of the road, pull out the mobile. Looks OK. Switched on already and plenty of battery. Glance round. I could do with another one. Many as I can get really. Check the time on the mobile.

Quarter to eight.

Shit, I've wasted fifteen minutes on this.

Stomach's churning, Bigeyes. I got to go. Forget about more mobiles. Got to hit the car and blow blood. Back down the street, past the alleyway, stop at the end, check faces. Round the corner, left again, down towards the shoe shop.

Jesus!

Two police cars parked further down. Four porkers standing in the street.

Checking my motor.

Slip behind a dustbin.

I'm stuffed, Bigeyes. I can't do this without a car. And I'm never going to find one at this late stage. But I got to hook one. Got to sort this gig today. I've made up my mind. It can't wait any longer.

Back to the end of the street. I'm desperate now. Yeah, I'm still scared. But I was fired up for this and I still am. Round the block, down to the alleyway. Stop, look round. There's got to be something, Bigeyes. There's got to be. I can't wait another day. And it's not just cos of me. It's cos one more day could be too late.

Cars ripping past, left and right. Christ, Bigeyes, everybody's got a motor except me. Then I clap him. Over the road. In the car park. Where the home used to be. And I've seen him before.

The old gobbo in his ancient car. He had a boy with him last time, about four years old. Looked like his grand-son. And there he is, in the passenger seat. They're getting out. Kid's running to the machine. Snaps the ticket, runs back. Gobbo's still heaving himself out of the car.

Got to go. Got to do this.

Over the road, into the car park. I'm pelting but I make myself slow down. If I freak 'em out, this won't work. Still might not cos I'm thinking bad and acting like a dimp. They've stuck the ticket on the windscreen and the old gobbo's locking the car.

Kid turns, sees me coming. Looks wary. I slow down to a walk, chuck him a smile. He doesn't look any happier. Bungs a glance at Grandad. The old gobbo turns, sees me.

'Good morning,' he says.

Still got the car keys in his hand. Gives me a smile.

'You look like you're in a hurry.'

Kid's still got that look on his face. It's putting me off.

I fix the old man, manage a smile back.

'Yeah, I'm a bit late. You couldn't tell me the time, could you?'

Gobbo slips the car keys in his pocket, glances at his watch.

'Ten to eight.'

I roll my eyes.

'Christ, I'm in trouble. Thanks a lot.'

I hurry forward.

'Good luck,' he says.

I slip past him, lift the keys from his pocket, walk on.

'Cheers, mate,' I call.

Keep walking, check over my shoulder. They're heading out of the car park. Gobbo looks relaxed. But the boy glances back one more time.

And then they're gone.

Back to the car, unlock it, jump in.

Heart's pounding again and I'm trembling bad. Check the clock. Seven minutes to eight. We're OK. We got time. Long as we don't get snagged with the traffic. Breathe slow, breathe slow. Got to calm down or I'll screw this gig.

Check round the car, make sure everything's cute.

Nice easy motor, nothing fancy. And look, Bigeyes. A little present.

He's left his mobile. Check it over. Jesus, what century did this thing come from? But it's switched on and I might need it. Pockets all bulging now but I shove it in.

Sit up, focus.

Take some more breaths.

Check I've got everything.

OK, OK.

And then suddenly it hits me. Something I wasn't ready for.

I'm fizzed up to go and in a couple more seconds I'll drive off and it'll start. But think for a moment, Bigeyes. Cos there's something else. I'm sitting on the site of the very place where everything started.

The home I first lived in.

The home that should never have been my home.

Or anyone else's.

And just for a moment, I feel it all again. Like I'm the same age as that boy who just bombed me with his look. I'm four years old again and I'm staring around me, and everything's burning, burning, burning.

Like I told you once before, Bigeyes.

Ghosts don't leave that easy.

Click on the belt, turn the key, rev up.

Out of the car park, into the road.

19 DOWN TO THE end, right at the lights. Speed steady. No need to rush. Traffic's moving.

Here's the street. Turn down it.

Remember, Bigeyes? We came this way, right at the start. Check round. What do you see? Cars, yeah, but what kind of cars? What do you see when you really look at 'em?

Money.

That's what you see. In this street all you see is money. More cars, lots of 'em. All the same. Lovely cars. With lovely kids inside 'em. Rich kids.

Here's the school. Remember it? Course you do.

Pull over, stay back. Perfect spot. Clear view of the main gate. Lots of kids in the playground already and more spilling in. Check out all the nebs. The beautiful people with their beautiful children, rolling up in their beautiful cars.

And here's the one I want.

All discreet.

No need to crow about being the richest family here. Everybody knows it, specially at one of the most expensive schools in the world. So it's a low-key Merc, if there is such a thing, and it's driven by the nanny. And the two grinks in the car behind are low-key too. Smart but not flash. Same gobbos as last time.

All discreet.

Can't believe how calm I've gone. Like all the tension's drained out now the gig's starting. But it won't be for long. Keep my eyes on the grinks. They're doing what they did last time. Keeping just behind.

But not too close. Everyone knows the boy in the Merc's got two bodyguards. But best not to upset the other parents. Cos some of 'em can't afford even one.

Yeah, grinks. Stay exactly where you are. Cos that's where I need you.

Fix the Merc. Two people in it. Damien and his nanny. She was better-looking in the old days. As for the boy . . .

I don't like watching him, Bigeyes.

He's six now but he was three when I ran away. Same age as Jaz is. And all I keep seeing is the face he had then. Only I can't bear to do it. Cos it's too much like hers.

Nanny pulls over. Grinks do the same just behind.

This is it.

I rev up, pull out, roar down the street, faster, faster.

Faces turn. Parents, teachers, kids, Nanny, Damien.

And now the grinks.

Both gobbos staring.

As I crash into the front of their car.

Shouts all around. My head's thumping. I braced myself ready for the impact but still got blammed. I kick the door open, stumble out of the car, blunder towards the Merc. Nanny and Damien are still in it, staring back at me. Nanny twists round, flicks on the central locking, revs up.

I grab the driver's door. Car starts to move off. I lose my grip, feel the car slip away. Grab the rear door, pull out the hammer, smash the glass, force up the lock. More shouts. Figures rushing close.

I yank the door open, throw myself into the back of the car, pull the door shut. Nanny slams on the brakes, screams at the boy.

'Get out the car! Get out the car!'

He doesn't move. He's frozen.

I whip out both knives, scramble between the front seats. Nanny tries to push me back but I thrust the blades at her face.

'Drive!' I bellow. 'Drive!'

She's not going to do it. She's staring at the blades, trying to hold out till help gets here. I see shadows close in on the car. I turn, dive on the boy, hold the knives over him. He screams. I bawl back at the woman.

'Drive or I'll cut him in two!'

She starts to drive, the boy still screaming under me.

'Faster!' I shout. 'Faster!'

She speeds up and now she's pulling clear. I check out

the window. It's teachers giving chase and one of the grinks. His mate's sprawled over the steering wheel of their motor.

Check the distance between us. I've got seconds to get away. They'll hit the cars any moment. Glance at Nanny. She's shaking but she's holding up, and she's watching close, like she's trying to think what to do.

It's got to be now.

'Pull over,' I snarl.

She pulls over. I spring at her.

'No!' she screams.

I force the knives back at her face.

'Out the car!' I yell.

'No!'

'Out the bloody car!'

She's edging back. Doesn't want to, but I'm pricking the blades into her neck. I reach out, open the driver's door.

'Get out!'

'Don't hurt the boy!'

'Get out!'

I kick her in the thigh. She tumbles into the street and rolls over the ground. I slam the door, rev up, blast off, check the mirror. Four gobbos thundering in. I put my foot down, hard. They fall back and vanish behind.

Don't look at me like that, Bigeyes.

Don't look at me at all.

Drive on, fast as I can without drawing attention.

This is it. My chance. The only one I'll get.

Left at the traffic lights. Going to head the wrong way and cut back. Try and confuse anyone who sees me. Past the alleyway, past the car park, right at the end, on to the roundabout, right again.

And now I look at the boy.

Been avoiding it all this time.

Never mind why.

He's not looking back. He's curled up in a ball, hiding his face. Dark smelly patch round his trousers where he's peed himself. And I'm wondering, Bigeyes. Is that what Jaz was like? When they took her? Eh? Got to keep wondering that. Keep remembering. Cos that's the only way I'll get through this.

Down to the junction, right at the end, now back on myself. And here it is. The lane between the offices. Nobody in it like before. And I don't think anyone's clapped us cutting in. Down to the end, left, and here's the garages.

All deserted.

Glance at the boy. Still curled up, not looking at me.

And he's crying now, whimpering.

Out of the car, open the garage door, drive in, engine off. Close the garage door, back in the car. Breathe, slow. Look down.

Both knives sitting on my lap.

Did I put 'em there just now? Was I holding 'em when I opened the garage door? Can't remember. Suppose I must have been. And put 'em back again afterwards without thinking. I stare at 'em, hate 'em.

Pick 'em up.

Feel Damien stiffen and watch.

I look round at him, put the knives back on my lap. Pull out the mobiles. Which one? Both dronky. But hang on. There's a third choice. Nanny's left hers in the Merc. What could be better?

Pick it up.

I already know the private number. Told you once before, Bigeyes. I remember stuff. But I don't need to remember this one. Cos Nanny's got it listed in her phone.

Lord H.

That's what it says. How cute is that? Well, it's a long surname. I don't blame her keeping it simple. Take another breath. Stare down at the phone.

Lord H.

Select. Press Dial.

Rings only once. Like I knew it would. And here's the voice.

Quiet, familiar.

'Yes?'

I don't answer. Don't need to. He knows exactly who it is. And what I want.

Damien goes on whimpering. I reach out the mobile, hold it close to him, let the sound weep into the phone. And for a moment I see that face again. Jaz's face, hanging there, like it did last night. Staring at me. I stare back, watch it fade.

Till all I see is Damien again, sobbing.

I pull the phone back, raise it, listen.
Silence at the other end. A waiting silence.
It's time to break it.
'Let's talk,' I say.

20

NOT A WORD from Lord H at the other end of the phone. And I know why. The bastard's waiting for me to speak. He knows I will. He knows I've got to. Cos he knows he's stronger than me.

I might have kidnapped his son, might have little Damien trembling next to me on the front seat of the car, freaking his head at the sight of my knives. But it makes no difference.

The silence goes on. Like a scream.

Cos Lord H is stronger than me.

Lord H.

Yeah, yeah.

I picture his face. He won't have changed at all. He'll be fifty-two now but he'll still look like he's forty. Younger even. An aristo god, master of all he surveys. Blue eyes, sculptured cheeks, hair the colour of a kiss.

If it wasn't for the mouth, you'd say it was a kind face.

And he can make it look kind when he wants to, even with the mouth. He can make it look anything. Only I know better. Cos I know the face too well.

Haven't seen it for three years, but I remember it good enough. The picture I usually get is me sprawled on my front and him peering down at me from on top. He's got a hand under my chin and my head yanked up so he can mock me in the eyes while he has his fun with me.

He liked that. Mocking, humiliating. There was nothing I could do to stop him. Cos the truth is, Bigeyes, he was just too strong. All I could do was keep telling myself no one could hurt me if I belonged to him.

But that was before Becky died.

And the whole world went quiet.

Like this phone in my hand. A small, quiet thing, its silence seeping into me. I can feel that power again, and it's not coming from me. It's coming from Lord H, like it's always done.

I got to fight it.

Somehow.

Glance at Damien. Kid's curled up on the passenger seat, eyes flicking over the knives on my lap. I speak into the phone.

'You know what I want.'

Still silence.

'And you know who I got here.'

I take a long, slow breath.

'You took Jaz. Or your goofs did. And I want her back.

So give her up and you get Damien. Simple as that. But listen.'

I take another breath. Got to keep my voice calm. Got to sound like I'm in control. Even if I'm not.

'You get what you give, OK? If Jaz is dead, then Damien's dead too.' I stare down at the knives. 'And so are the rest of your kids.'

Damien starts sobbing again.

Yeah, I know. I hate doing this, Bigeyes, but I got no choice. There's too much at stake now. So I got to play it rough.

I can't mess with this slime. He wants his boy back but he's cold as steel and twice as hard. And that's not the worst. The worst is he's clever. Cleverer than anyone you'll ever meet. And more ruthless.

Don't be deceived like everybody else.

'Here's how it's going to work,' I say.

Still the silence. It's deeper than ever now. I can feel his hatred churning inside it, cold and dark. I force myself to go on.

'You get your goofs to drive Jaz to the police station. The one in New Cross Road. They stop outside, leave her by the main entrance, drive off. Someone'll be waiting for her.'

I pick up one of the knives.

'When I hear she's safe, I'll ring you again. And tell you where you can find Damien.'

Wait, listen.

He's never going to buy this. He's going to want a

straight swap, both kids together. That way he's got a chance of slamming me too. He'll never hand over Jaz and take my word I'll ring him about Damien afterwards.

'You got an hour,' I mutter. 'An hour from now.' I check the car clock. 'If she's not at the station by ten, I'll take it she's dead. And you know what that means for Damien.'

I squeeze the knife tight.

'And in case you're wondering, cos some of your slugs might just have told you I've lost my bottle, there's something you got to know. I'm not going to kill Damien myself. I'm going to hand him over to less pleasant people.'

I pause.

'Like Nelson or Fitz or Jimmy-Joe Spice. Or one of the others. There's plenty of bojos who'd like a piece of your kid. If you think I'm bluffing, try me.'

Damien starts wailing nearby.

Still silence down the phone. Freaking me bad now, Bigeyes. Cos I can't work out what he's thinking. I could once. Or I thought I could. But not any more. Then it happens.

The click at the other end of the line.

And he's gone.

Lean back in the driver's seat. I'm shivering. Trying not to but I can't stop. Got to do something, get a grip. Can't let Damien see me scared. Check him out. He hasn't noticed what I'm like. He's still wailing and he's turned away again, his face pressed against the side window of the car.

I stare past him at the garage wall beyond.

This isn't going to work, Bigeyes.

Lord Slime's never going to do what I want. And maybe he can't anyway. If Jaz is already dead, what can he do? On the other hand, what if Jaz is alive? There's still just a chance. And I got to act like there is.

Cos there's not much else I can do.

'Damien,' I say.

He doesn't answer, doesn't turn. Just keeps on crying, face against the window. I don't blame him. Jaz must have been the same. Blasted out of her head. But I don't want to think about that.

'Damien, I'm not going to kill you.'

Or hand him over, Bigeyes. Before you ask. I never intended to give him up to Nelson or the other gangsters. But I can't tell him that now. I just want him to stop crying. First cos I got to make another call and I don't want the sound spilling down the phone. And second . . .

Cos I just want him to.

He curls up tight, hands clasped over the back of his head. But the crying eases off, turns into a sniffle. I can handle that. Look down at the mobile, punch in the number. Funny how it comes back. Like all the other numbers. Don't ask me how I do it, cos I don't know. I just remember stuff.

Press Dial.

Ring, ring.

He better bloody answer. It's not a whack like it was with Lord H. Slimeface was always going to pick up the phone. But this one's different. Still, I got a couple of backup numbers if the call doesn't work.

Ring, ring.

Come on.

Ring ring. Answerphone kicks in. Grumpy voice. Hasn't changed.

'Inspector Bannerman—'

'Yeah, yeah.'

'I'm not at my desk right now—'

'Lazy bastard.'

'But if you leave your name and contact details after the beep—'

I hang up, key in another number.

Ring, ring. This one's his mobile. Let's hope he's—

Shit. Voicemail.

'Bannerman speaking. Can't take your call right now but if you—'

Hang up, glance at Damien, back at the phone. Last number I got. Key it in.

Ring, ring.

'Hello?'

Woman's voice. Wasn't expecting that. Maybe he's moved. Cos I mean, there was no way he was ever going to get a wife. Not with a face like that. But maybe he's got a sister.

'Who is this?' she says.

I know that voice, Bigeyes. I've heard it before.

'Haven't got all day,' she says.

I make myself speak.

'Is Inspector Bannerman there?'

'*Inspector* Bannerman?' she says.

'Yeah.'

'Is this a police matter?'

'Might be.'

'Because if it is,' she goes on, 'you should be ringing the police station, not here. This is a private number.'

And suddenly I get it, Bigeyes. The voice. And I can't believe it. I can picture her face, clear as his, clear as my own in the car mirror. But it's not her face I remember most about her. It's something else. Something big.

Bosoms.

That's what I remember.

And that's what I called her. When I was seven. What the hell's she doing answering his private phone? It can't be what I'm thinking. No way. Not with him.

'Ring the station,' she snaps.

'It's Jonny Bell,' I say.

Intake of breath at the other end. I can feel her thinking. She was about to hang up. She still is. Don't ask me how I know. Sound of a door somewhere near her, footsteps coming close. Someone muttering, Bosoms whispering back, then a new voice in my ear. A new, old voice.

'Jonny Bell,' it says.

'Inspector Bannerman.'

He gives a sneery chuckle.

'Or are we Billy Nail today? Or Richie Finch? Or Jimmy Stoko? Or Frankie Reeve or Stevie Black or—'

'Going through the whole list, are you?'

'Don't suppose I know the whole list,' says Bannerman. 'And even if I did, there's not much point reading it off. Life's too short for your fantasies. So let's keep it simple. Why don't I just call you Blade?'

'Yeah, why don't you?'

I give a sneery chuckle of my own.

'Pugface.'

21

BANNERMAN SNORTS.

'Pugface? That your name for me? I think you can do better than that.'

'I got others.'

'I bet you have.' He sniffs. 'So how did you get my home number?'

'I've always had it.'

'You never used it before.'

'Don't tell me you're disappointed.'

Bannerman grunts.

'So what's this about? Giving yourself up?'

'No.'

'You should. It's pointless running.'

'You got to help someone.'

'Who?'

'A three-year-old girl. She's called Jaz. She's—'

'I know who she is,' says Bannerman. 'And I know about

Rebecca Jakes. And Trixi Kenton. And her brother Dig. And all the others. Including the elderly Irish woman.'

I feel myself stiffen.

'Mary,' I murmur.

'Yes.'

I swallow hard.

'Is she . . . I mean . . . is she still alive?'

'I don't have any information about her.'

'Cos last time I saw her, she was really ill. She was—'

'I don't have any information about her.'

Silence. I don't know what I feel. Just know it hurts. Like thinking about Becky hurts. Bannerman goes on.

'How can I help the little girl?'

His voice sounds sharp, like he wants me to hurry on. And I'm glad. Cos I want to hurry on too. Can't be thinking about Mary. Not right now. There's no time to waste.

'You got to move quick,' I tell him. 'You and what's her name?'

'Who?'

I can't say Bosoms, Bigeyes. Even to Bannerman.

'Who?' he says.

'The woman who answered the phone.'

'DI Fern?'

'Yeah. You got to ring the station. Right now. Tell 'em Jaz is going to be dropped outside the main entrance some time before ten.'

'How do you know?'

'Never mind. I don't know what state she'll be in but it's going to be bad. They're not to mess with the people leaving her there. Probably won't get a chance. They'll drive off quick. But someone's got to be there to look after Jaz.'

Bannerman doesn't answer but I hear him muttering to Fern. Can't catch the words but I hear her say, 'OK.' Nothing for a bit, then I catch Fern's voice talking on another phone. And here's Bannerman back.

'Now then,' he begins.

But I cut him short.

'You got to get there too, Bannerman. You and Fern.'

'There'll be people waiting at the station.'

'I want you there. And Fern.'

'We can't get there right away.'

'You got to be there. Both of you. For when Jaz turns up.'

'What for?'

Because she's got to meet the right nebs, Bigeyes. It can't just be anyone waiting for her. I'm not mad on porkers at the best of times, but I got time for Bannerman. And if Fern's his squeeze or his mate or whatever, that's even better. Cos she's decent too.

They'll help Jaz.

And that's all I care about.

'Never mind why,' I mutter. 'Get to the station and I'll ring you later.'

'Why don't you just come in?'

'Why don't you just shut your mouth?'

I hang up, lean back again. Shivering like before. Not so bad as with Lord H, but I'm choked, Bigeyes. Head's full of stuff I can't handle. And now they're back again. Bloody tears. They're swilling round my eyes and I can't stop 'em.

And worse.

I'm moaning, shaking, slamming my head with my fists. Damien's peering round, his own eyes drenched up, his mouth gaping as he stares at me. I stare back, try to get a grip.

But I can't. The tears keep flooding, then something bursts out of me, a kind of bellow. Can't hold it back. I feel my hands clutch the knives, squeeze. I close my eyes and howl into the dark.

Feels like ages before I stop. When I do, I realize I've curled into a ball just like Damien did before. I can feel it, even with my eyes still closed. I've got my knees pulled into my chest, my hands clasped round the ankles. Must have let go the knives cos they're tucked into my lap, and the top of my head's pressed against the steering wheel. I can feel it chafing against the wound in my brow.

I keep my eyes closed a bit longer. Don't want to open 'em. Not yet. I take a long breath. Feels juddery, like my lungs don't want to work. Take another breath. Just as hard. Open my eyes, look round.

Damien's not there.

I stiffen. Passenger door's open, no sign of the kid. I feel a flutter of panic, grab the knives, scramble out of the car—and there's the boy. Far corner of the garage, slumped against the wall.

Never heard him get out. I must have been in a bad

state to miss that. He could have got away maybe, if he'd had the spit. But he's still too scared. He looks up, watches me standing by the car, shrinks closer to the wall.

I call over.

'I'm not angry with you.'

He doesn't answer. Just goes on watching, his face dark.

And I'm wondering, Bigeyes. Does he see my darkness too? He must. He's seen me break down, heard me moan and howl and sob. He can't be scared of me still, can he?

But he is. Look at him.

Choked out of his wits.

Maybe he thinks I'm even more dangerous now I've cracked in front of him. And maybe he's right. Maybe I am more dangerous. Truth is, Bigeyes, I don't know what I am any more. Or what I can do.

I used to know. Used to be bung-clear about all that.

And it gave me confidence.

Now I got none.

'I'm not angry with you,' I say again.

Don't know why I'm repeating myself. He just looks more scared every time I open my mouth. I look down. Still holding the knives, see? Same old problem. Like my hands are magnets. I grabbed the bastards without thinking.

Look back at Damien. Still watching me.

With those dark little eyes.

I drop the knives on the seat, close the door, edge round the front of the car towards the boy. He starts to whimper, press himself back against the wall. I stop moving, call out.

'Easy, kid.'

He goes on whimpering.

'Easy, kid.' I sit down on the bonnet, look down at him. 'I'm not going to hurt you.'

He keeps his eyes on my face.

I stare at him. Hard to think this boy's got such a father. If only he knew what his dad's really like. But he won't have a sniff of that. How could he? How could anyone? Cos you know what?

Only a handful of nebs know what Lord H really is. His wife and children certainly won't. Nor will his relatives, or his friends. Or the nebs who run his charities. They only see the caring family man, the great public benefactor.

And one of the richest guys on the planet. He was already that when he was born. Only it wasn't enough, Bigeyes. He's a business supergun too and he must have earned his inheritance twenty times over.

But let's give the bastard his name. And Nanny keyed it pretty good in her mobile—Lord H. Which kind of hits the spot. Only there's something about the H Nanny won't realize.

It hits the spot twice.

First there's the name she knows. The official name.

Lord Haffler-Devereaux.

Yeah, I agree. Fancy prick of a name. But don't worry. We don't need to use that. Not you and me, Bigeyes. Cos he's got another name. Another H name. And Nanny won't know that one. Practically nobody will, not even his wife, or his kids, or the thousands who work for him, or the government nebs who listen to his advice.

It's a name only the other slimeheads know. The ones at the top of his organization. The handful, the chosen few. The puppet-masters who are slowly cutting the cords that hold this world together. The ones behind the charade.

I told you about it before.

The Game.

They all got names, these players. Secret names for their secret lives. Want to hear 'em? Then listen. And remember.

Raven, Swan, Swift, Owl, Condor.

And then our man—Lord H. Worked out the H? Course you have.

Hawk.

That's what the other slimeheads call him.

And it fits pretty good. Cos you know what? For all his looks, charm, and manners, that's what he is. He roams like a hawk, sees like a hawk, kills like a hawk. And you never know he's there till it's too late.

I feel Damien's eyes on me. Stare back at 'em. Is that Hawk looking out at me? A future Hawk? Who's to know? Can't see one now. All I can see is a scared kid. He wipes his eyes and drops his head.

I reach into my pocket, feel for one of the mobiles, pull it out. It's the one I creamed off that ancient gobbo in the car park. Dimpy old phone. But who cares? Long as it works.

Too early to ring the police station. Jaz can't possibly be there yet. If she's going to turn up at all. But I can't help it, Bigeyes. I got to try Bannerman again. It's just possible.

Punch in the number. I'm trying his mobile first. He won't have hit the station yet but someone might have rung him already with some news.

Ring, ring.

This is stupid. It's much too early to phone. I got to be patient.

Click.

'Bannerman speaking.'

'It's Blade.'

'What do you want?'

'Any news of Jaz?'

'Give us a chance. We've only just left the house.'

I can hear the sound of the car. And Fern talking in the background. Jesus, Bigeyes. What's she saying? Who's she talking to? Can't catch the words. It better be someone from the station. It better be good news.

'Ring me later,' says Bannerman. 'I'm driving. Or better still, come in to the station.'

'Piss off.'

'Suit yourself.'

Sound of a car horn, a growl from Bannerman. Fern still mumbling in the background.

'I'm hanging up,' says Bannerman. 'Ring me later.'

'Wait!' Fern's voice nearby. 'Hold on!'

More muttering, one to the other, then Fern's voice in the earpiece.

'Are you there?' she says.

'Yeah.'

I stare back at Damien. He's watching me close again. And suddenly I see it, just for a moment, in those small, six-year-old eyes. The hawk, peering back.

Marking prey.

Though he doesn't know it yet.

Fern speaks again. And there's a shiver in her voice.

'They've got Jaz.'

22 I FEEL THE words rush out of me.

'Is she alive? Is she alive?'

'She's . . . alive,' says Fern.

She hesitated, Bigeyes. Did you hear that? She definitely hesitated. And she spoke quiet. Something's wrong. I slam in quick.

'What's happened?'

'I just told you,' says Fern. 'She's alive.'

'You hesitated!'

'Don't shout down the phone.'

'I'm not shouting!'

But I am, Bigeyes. I can't help it. I got to know what Fern's holding back.

'Tell me!' I bellow. 'What have they done to her?'

Silence at the other end. I see Damien staring up at me, mouth open. Fern answers, same quiet voice.

'I don't know what state she's in. I haven't got any details.

We're still on our way to the station. I just know she's alive.'

'But you hesitated!'

'I hesitated because of you.'

I clench my fists, try to understand. But it won't come. I'm so fizzed about Jaz, about wanting to know she's OK, I can't think straight. Fern speaks again.

'I hesitated because of you.'

'What about me?'

'You surprised me.'

'Eh?'

Bannerman takes over the phone.

'You surprised her. And me.'

'I wasn't talking to you, Bannerman.'

'You were shouting so loud down the phone you were talking to both of us.'

I don't answer.

'And we were both surprised,' he goes on.

'What about?'

'You caring for the girl.'

'What's wrong with that?'

'Nothing. We just didn't think you were capable of it.'

'Capable of what?'

'Caring.'

His words stab me. I catch Damien still watching, look away towards the side wall. Can't bear the sight of his eyes, not when I'm trying to get my head round this other stuff.

Not capable of caring.

Not capable.

So what about Becky? Eh? What about Mary? I care for them. Not bloody capable. I feel the tears start again. Cos the trouble is, Bigeyes—Bannerman's right. Deep down I know it. I didn't use to care. Not till I met Becky. And when she died, I stopped again. Till now. But Bannerman won't know that. Nor will Fern. Or anyone else.

Why should they?

He speaks again, hard voice.

'Come into the station. Come now. It's the right thing. And we'll let you see Jaz.'

'Yeah, right,' I mutter. 'Before you take her away.'

'Do you expect us to keep her for you?'

I don't answer.

'Eh?' he says. 'You must have known this was going to happen when you fixed for her to get dropped at the station. And you did fix that, didn't you? It's not an accident. Or something you just happened to know about. You fixed it, didn't you?'

I still don't answer. But he's right about Jaz. Course he is. I always knew what was going to happen. Thing is, Bigeyes, what else could I do? Jaz can't live with Bex. And she certainly can't live with me. Or the troll-gang from the old city. Bex won't be pleased but she'll have to deal with it.

And so will I.

But I still can't bear the thought of never seeing her again.

'She's not yours,' says Bannerman. 'Are you listening? You're not her father or her brother or her guardian.'

'Piss off.'

'She doesn't belong to you. And she doesn't belong to Rebecca Jakes. If you've helped get her to the police station, that's good. It's a mark in your favour. But that's all. She's not yours to keep. It's for other people to take over now. There's a system in place to help kids like her.'

'Yeah, sure. Like the system that helped me.'

There's a pause. Think he's handed the phone back to Fern. Yeah, he has. Here's her voice again.

'Are you there?'

I don't answer.

'Come in to the station,' she says. 'You can't stay on the run for ever. Give yourself up.'

She's talking gentle, like she's coaxing. Makes me think of Mary. Mary told me to give myself up too. And I was going to, remember? Had it sorted in my head. Before the grinks took Jaz. And killed Dig.

Maybe that's what's waiting for me, Bigeyes.

A knife through the heart. Like he got.

Glance back at Damien. And for another small moment, I see that look in his face. Yeah, yeah, he's still what he was—a frightened kid. Yet somewhere in those scared little eyes I can see the hunter that'll come looking for me one day.

If his dad doesn't get me first.

'I'm not giving myself up,' I mutter.

And hang up.

Silence again. Feels so deep I'm scared it's going to swallow me. I listen for sounds outside. There they are—cars, smellies, stuff. The hum of the Beast as the world wakes from another misty sleep.

I look at Damien.

Still watching me.

Still scared.

If only he knew how scared I am of him.

I walk over to him, look down. His eyes widen, his mouth gapes. I want to speak to him. Say I'm sorry. But I can't. I turn away, edge back to the driver's door, reach in.

Pull out the knives.

Feel Damien stiffen again.

I straighten up, call out.

'Sorry.'

He's crying again, quietly now, not sobbing or whimpering like he was before. Just soft little tears, running down his face. I turn away, listen cute, ease up the garage door.

Light dribbles in, grizzly and grey. Spit of breeze brushes over me. Check round. No nebs to be seen but I can feel plenty near. Got to wig it while I got a chance. Find somewhere safe. Where I can think.

But first things first.

Check inside the garage again. Damien's still slumped on the floor. He's staring out at me round the side of the motor. I call back to him.

'Stay where you are, OK?'

He doesn't answer.

'Stay where you are till they come and get you. Don't walk off on your own. And don't open the garage door.'

What the hell am I doing worrying about this kid? I shouldn't give two bells about him. But I can't be dealing with that now. Swing down the garage door, check round again.

Down to the lane, stop, glance round it.

All clear.

I know what I want to do, Bigeyes. Blast out, run my feet off. But it's no good. There's something else I got to do first. Dimpy and risky, but I can't stop myself. Check down the lane.

Remember what I told you about those buildings? They're offices. Crumbly, useless offices. I used to bust in there sometimes when I had to slap it for a night or two.

Well, I'm busting in again. Only not for the night.

Down the lane, checking cute. Got to be dead careful cos I haven't been here for three years. I don't know what's in these places any more. They haven't been tarted up. Anyone can see that. But I haven't grubbed out the inside.

So keep your eyes open.

First gate, check round. Nobody in the lane, nobody on the other side. I reckon this building's deserted. Going to risk it anyway. Over the railing, into the courtyard, round the back to the door.

Just like it used to be.

Tatty and tired.

Listen cute.

Not a sound inside. Creep past the windows, check through. Empty rooms. Check over my shoulder. Lost the hammer when I jacked Nanny's car but this brick'll do.

Pick it up, wait, listen. Smash!

Glass breaks easy. No sound of an alarm. Flick the catch, inch up the window, squeeze through, listen again. Still silence. Just the traffic noise beyond the lane.

And my heart pounding in my chest.

Through the downstairs rooms, soft, slow, listening cute. Not a sound inside the building, just my steps padding on the dry wooden boards. No furniture in any of the rooms, but there's paint pots, brushes and cloths at the bottom of the stairs. Someone's got plans for this place, that's clear.

Let's just hope they don't turn up for a bit.

Least this won't take long.

Up the stairs, slow, soft, checking round. First floor. More paint pots, brushes in jars, cloths and buckets, overalls. Packet of cigs, open, half-full.

Stop, listen.

Still silence.

Up the next flight of stairs. It's coming back to me, Bigeyes. Must have been eight or nine when I last came in here. But I still recognize the place, even without the desks and filing cabinets.

Second floor. Wallpaper peeling all round. Down to the landing. There used to be one last flight of stairs. There you go, behind that door. Little stairway to the top of the building.

And that's what I want.

You'll soon see why.

Up the stairs, into the little room, over to the window, kneel down. Got to keep low. No curtain to hide round and it's easy to be seen from down below. But it's a good view the other way too. Check it out, Bigeyes.

What do you see below?

The garages.

Perfect place to look down. Just got to make sure I keep myself well hidden. Let's go. Pull out the phone. I'm using Nanny's mobile again.

Scroll down.

Lord H.

Dial.

He won't speak at all this time, Bigeyes. I'm telling you. He won't even say 'Yes?' Which is fine by me.

Click.

He answers first ring. And there it is.

Silence.

'Listen good,' I say. 'Cos I'm not saying it twice.'

I tell him where the boy is, stop, wait. Don't know why. I told you, Bigeyes, he's not going to speak. I don't even want him to. I just . . . I don't know . . . want him to feel I'm not scared. Like I'm cute with the silence.

Except I'm not.

It's freaking me already.

Like before.

I hang up, drop the mobile on the floor, stamp it to bits. Slump on the boards, wait. It won't take long. They'll be here in minutes. And so will he. That's right, Bigeyes. He'll come personally. I know it.

He'll be here in ten.

23 HE'S HERE IN five. There's a sound of motors, big, powerful beasts. I straighten up, edge to the window, slow, careful. Got to play it cute. I'm pretty sure they won't be looking for me up here. They'll think I've blasted out, fast as I can, far as I can.

Even so.

Got to be careful.

Straighten up, slow, slow. I'm keeping to the side of the window this time, not peeping from underneath. Check down. Four motors parked outside the garages.

One of 'em's his.

Gobbos spilling out of the cars. Six, seven, eight, nine. Big dronks, shiny suits, groomed. Upper-class grinks, not the sluggy low-life that first caught up with me. But what else do you expect? The Hawk's never going to look cheap.

Why hasn't he got out?

I'm fixing his motor. You bet I am. Check it out, Bigeyes. Even the car's an aristo. It's purring with the engine off. Two figures still in it. Driver in the front, Hawk in the back. Or just the shadow of him.

Cos he's sitting far side, behind the passenger seat, head turned away. Get out, you slime. I want to see you again. I want to stick your evil face. Not cos I need to. But cos I want to.

Cos you're my enemy.

The biggest one I ever had. Or ever will.

And that's saying something, considering how many I got.

But he's still sitting there. Lets his grinks buzz over to the garage, yank up the door, bomb inside. Out again, one of 'em holding the kid. And now here's Daddy. Door of the car's opened, and he's out in the open.

At last.

Arms wide, takes the boy, hugs him close, face buried in Damien's neck, other side of the kid's face, so I still can't see what I want. All I got is the boy's cheek. He's crying. I can see from here. Crying his head off.

Gobbos edge round close. Hawk waves 'em off, mutters something. One of 'em trigs back into the garage, starts up Nanny's car, backs it out. The others spread out, check round the garages, over by the wall, back towards the lane.

Towards me.

I inch to the side of the window.

Jesus, don't tell me they're grubbing out this place. I

never thought they would. Glance round the window, just a peep. They've stopped at the lane. Think they're just checking round, making sure all's cute for the Hawk. Not looking for me special.

Yeah, I'm right.

They're heading back to the motors. Getting in, doors closing, engines revving up. Only the Hawk's still standing there, Damien pressed close. Boy's still crying, Daddy stroking the back of his head. And now he's bending down, handing the boy in to one of the gobbos in the car.

And then he straightens up. Looks over.

At me.

Only he can't see me. No way. Not from there. I'm peeping round so I can clap him but there's just a shiver of me outside the window-frame. No way he can see me. No bloody way.

But I can see him.

I can see him good, Bigeyes.

Check out the face. Go on. Do it. Hair, cheeks, mouth, eyes. You can see all of 'em from here, even the eyes. OK, maybe not the eyes. Maybe I'm just remembering the eyes. But I can see the rest. And so can you.

Remember what I said? How young he looks? Ten years, twenty years younger than he is. Not that I give two bells. It doesn't matter how old he is. All that matters is how dangerous he is.

And how few nebs know that.

Or will ever believe it.

That's the problem, Bigeyes.

Cos you're looking at Mr Good. Mr Squeaky Clean. Philanthropist, Patron of the Arts, Public Benefactor, Collector and Connoisseur of Beautiful Things.

Remember that face, Bigeyes. Keep it in your head. Let it burn into you. Like it's burned into me. I hoped I'd never see it again. But I guess I was a dimp. I was always going to. And anyway, why bother about hope?

When hope's never bothered about me.

He's still looking up. Just standing there, gazing. He can't know. He can't. If he'd seen me, he'd never just stand there. He'd have his dronks snapped round the building by now, blocking the exits, crashing in. I'd be dung by now.

If he knew.

He can't have seen me.

He can't have guessed.

But he's still standing there, looking up. And I'm staring back, hidden—surely. Just the smallest part of me in his sight line, too small, too far, just the edge of one eye for him to see. He can't clap that from there.

But he still hasn't moved.

Cars nosing round him. Check that out, Bigeyes. He's just standing there, making no room. And the big motors are creeping round him. That's power. He doesn't move for anyone. Never has done, never will. They can hardly get past without brushing him or knocking him, one side or the other.

And still he won't move for 'em.

Glances round at the nearest car. I miss the look. Can't see it with his head flicked away. But I clap the face of the driver. Yeah, mate. You're sweating, right? Cos the boss just shot one at you with his eyes.

And I know what it said.

Mess my suit and you're mince.

Car slinks past him. Others follow, crab round into the lane, stop, wait. Hawk takes no notice of 'em. Turns his head, back to me, walks forward, closer, closer, stops again, just under my window. I edge to the side, right out of view.

He can't see me now, definitely. But I can't see him either. And I don't like that. Wait, pressed against the wall, heart thumping, blood racing. Listen. Listen good. Going to be one of two sounds. Engines or a smash of glass. If it's the first, I'm cute. If it's the second, I'm finished.

Smash of glass.

I stiffen, reach for the knives, squeeze 'em tight.

Then another sound.

Engines.

And a car door slamming shut. Just one. It better be his. Jesus, Bigeyes, it better be his. Revving up, squeal of tyres, and they're pulling away. I tighten my grip on the knives, ease out so I can see through the window. Got to risk it. Got to make sure it's not a trick.

But they're going.

All the motors. And Hawk's going with 'em. I can see the back of his head as the car slips away. He's got his arm round Damien and he's cuddling the boy close. The kid looks back, just once, and I stiffen again.

But then he twists round again, tucks his head into Daddy's shoulder.

And they're gone.

I breathe out, slow, hard. Heart's still pumping. Got to check round. Make sure it's still safe. This could be a trap. He might just have clapped me up here and let a couple of his grinks sneak round to hide and pick me up on the way out.

And somebody definitely smashed a window.

Down the stairs, soft, cute. Check round, every space, every shadow. All quiet in the building. Not even a creak of the boards. Check each floor, down to the next, down to the bottom, stop.

Check again.

Listen.

Nobody. Creep round the downstairs rooms, check out the windows into the lane. Clear so far. Front room—broken glass all over the floor. Old nobbly brick lying there. He must have flobbed it in, Bigeyes.

The Hawk.

I reckon he just did. Cos he's raging. Cos he wants my blood.

And he never knew I was here. Lucky me.

Slip the knives away, bend down, pick up the brick. Squeeze it tight. Turn and fling it against the far wall. It thunders back at me, bounces on the floor, lies still. I stare down at it.

Cos suddenly I know, Bigeyes. Suddenly it's clear. This is where we find out—who's the hunter, who's the prey. I'm raging too. I want blood too. I'm not leaving. I know that now. Not wigging it out of the Beast.

First cos I got to check Jaz is cute. Check she's looked after good. Even if I can't see her again, I got to make sure she's OK. And second cos there's things about the past I want to put right.

Right as I can anyway.

And there's something else too. Something big.

I got my enemy. Got him fixed in my head. He was there before, course he was, but now I've seen him again, he's clearer than ever. And I know this for certain.

I can't run any more. You know why? Cos he'll never rest till he's found me. Till I'm dust trickling through his hands. So I got one choice left. Bring him down.

That's right, Bigeyes.

I got to mix it.

24

I PULL OUT the old gobbo's mobile, stab in the number, wait.

'Yeah?' says Ruby.

'It's me.'

She gives a grunt.

'How you get this number?'

'I remembered it.'

'I never give it you.'

'Becky did.'

'That don't make it right.'

'Can I speak to Bex?' I say.

'No.'

'Why not?'

'She gone.'

'Gone?'

'You heard me.'

'Where?'

'How do I know?'

Click of the phone as she hangs up. Silence again. Just my thoughts cracking my head. And the drone of traffic beyond the lane. I try the number again. Rings and rings, then she picks it up.

'Don't got nothing to say to you.'

'Ruby—'

'Piss off.'

'Meet me in the alley behind The Turk's Head.'

'I don't hang about in alleys. Not no more.'

'It's about Becky.'

She doesn't answer.

'It's about Becky,' I say.

I see that face again. That beautiful black face. Like I'm staring at the photo in Ruby's shrine. And somehow the real face is smiling back. Like it always did.

Except at the end.

I try to take a breath. Won't come. Feels like the air's fighting me, like it thinks I don't deserve it. Maybe I don't. I try again, gulp in a bit.

'Ruby, listen. I want to tell you what happened to her.'

'Tell me now,' she snaps. 'We don't need no alleyway.'

'I want to show you where it happened. And . . . I want to explain.'

She's quiet again. Still raging. She wants me dead so much. And I don't blame her.

'I didn't kill Becky,' I tell her. 'I promise I didn't. But . . . '

I hesitate.

'But what?' she growls.

'It's my fault she died.'

Ruby starts to sniffle.

'Ruby, listen—'

'Leave me alone.'

'Meet me behind The Turk's Head.'

'You bastard!'

I squeeze the phone tight.

'Ruby,' I mutter, 'I know you hate me, but . . .'

It's no good, Bigeyes. The words won't come. I can feel 'em freezing in my mouth. I want to put things right, I swear I do, but talking's no good now. It's too late for that. Becky's dead and nothing'll bring her back.

Ruby speaks suddenly, grit-hard.

'I'll meet you.'

'OK. Midnight.'

'No,' she slams. 'Not midnight. Now!'

'It's got to be midnight. I can't get there before.'

Yeah, I know. I'm lying, Bigeyes. I can get there before. But there's a reason why it's got to be midnight. First cos I got other stuff to do. And second—well, never mind. It's just got to be midnight, OK?

'Alley behind The Turk's Head,' I say. 'Midnight.'

Ruby hangs up without a word.

Out of the door, round the building, back to the lane. Got to blast out of this place now, wig it fast. Hawk's gone but his grinks'll be close, and they might just lick over this patch first.

Makes sense. Last place they know I was, so they'll probably sling a net round it and squeeze just in case. I've smacked it here long enough. Over the gate, into the lane. Check right and left.

Two motors parked down the far end where it meets the main street. They don't look like trouble but that means nothing. Check the other way. Garages look clear and I can always cut back the way I want to go.

Come on, Bigeyes.

Over the lane, down to the garages. Stop, flick a glance round. Looks cute. End of the row, last garage, stop again, check round. Scraggy grass down to the far wall, nobody in sight.

Round the garage, over the scrub, stop at the wall, listen. Traffic drumming past on the other side. Bit of a risk now, me suddenly appearing on top of the wall. Some driver might chuck a glint. I might even cop a grink ripping past at just the wrong moment.

But I got to go for it.

Scramble up. Brick's kind of crumbly but it's got plenty of holds and it should do. Up to the top, peer over. Taxis, bikes, motors, smellies. Wait for a gap, scramble over, jump down the other side, turn my face to the wall. Drone of engines goes on behind me. Pull up the hood, saunter down the road, face low. Catch the front of a bonnet in the corner of my eye.

Just appeared, moving slow, like it's tracking me.

Keep my face down, turned away, but not right to the wall. Got to keep half a glance on the motor. It's still there, keeping pace with me. I slow right down. It still won't cut off, just eases down, like it's stuck to me.

I stop.

It does the same.

I turn, fix it. Big motor, flash, four gobbos in it, all suits. Passenger window rolls down, guy leans out, shouts over.

'Know where Duke Street is?'

'First right, third left.'

'Cheers, kid.'

And they're gone.

Walk on, slow, hood still up, checking cute. I'm going the same way as those gobbos, only further. Whip a glance back over the traffic. Might risk a smelly if it looks safe. Or a taxi.

Got to watch good though. The grinks'll be buzzing their eyes over everything and they're going to be even more snicky now I've roughed Hawk's kid.

Over the road, first right, past the engineering works, check round. Couple of taxis. Both taken. Three more. Same again. Walk on. Smelly rumbling the other way. Trig past the parade of shops, cross over.

Another smelly. Coming up behind. Number 34.

This'll do. Long as it's safe. Run down to the stop, huddle round to the back of the queue, keep low. Peer out at the bus. Packed full. Got nebs standing down the middle. Don't like the look of 'em, Bigeyes. Might be wrong but I'm not risking it.

Doors open. Passengers pile off, my lot pile on.

Stay back, watch.

Still don't like the look of 'em.

Walk on down the street. Just didn't feel right. Didn't

clap anybody. But you can't always tell grinks. I'm speed-
ing up. Can't help myself. I feel edgy. This is bad, Bigeyes.
I'm just feeling more and more scared. It's the Beast making me choke.

I keep thinking of the old city. She was tough and she
could scare me too.

But she wasn't like the Beast. She had some kindness
in her. Places I could go and feel safe. Not here. Every
street's going to be like this. Even when there's no grink
in sight. Sound of footsteps behind me. Running.

Following.

I jump over to the wall, twist round, hood still up.

Two dronks racing towards me. Black kids. Sixteen,
seventeen. Dreads, glitter. No question they got blades. I
brace myself, reach for the knives, hold 'em ready, under
my coat. The dronks bomb close.

And run past.

Didn't fix me once.

Neither of 'em.

Smelly drums past a moment later. Still packed with
nebs. And somehow they look different now. Older. Like
they're pensioners. Dunnies, half of 'em, naffing like
they're on an outing. A little jaunt. Off to the zoo maybe.
Or one of the sights.

One happy little smelly.

Disappears like the two black dronks.

What's happening to me, Bigeyes?

I'm jumping at everything.

Walk. Got to keep walking, keep moving. Stuff to do,

whether I'm freaked or not. Shift your stump. Move, move, move.

Down the street, hugging the wall. Hands tight round the knives under my coat. Try to ease the fingers free. They don't want to let go. They want to cling on. They won't let go.

Jesus, Bigeyes. I don't know what's right any more.

I feel scared with the knives and just as scared without 'em.

Still clutching the hilts.

'Let go.'

I'm muttering aloud. Hear that, Bigeyes? That's how bad I'm getting.

'Let go.'

'Stop talking to yourself.'

And now I'm muttering back. Both ways. Speaking and answering. Jesus, I'm clapping myself over.

'Stop talking to yourself.'

'Shut up!'

Still doing it. Still bloody doing it.

Take a breath, walk on, take another breath, walk on. Step, breathe, step, breathe. And I'm still holding the eff-ing blades.

'Let go of 'em!'

Shouting now. Blasting out the words. Or they're blast-ing out of me. Can't stop 'em.

'Let go! Let go!'

Gobbo on the far pavement bobs a glance. I fix him heavy. He turns away, hurries on, doesn't look back. Walk

on, walk on. I'm like a dead weight. This is so bad, Bigeyes.
I got no chance mixing it with the Hawk if I'm nicked in
the head.

Got to get a grip. Make myself calm down. Stop, wait,
take another breath. Let go of the knives. Let go of the
bloody knives.

Done it.

Thank Christ.

Pull my hands out, flick the fingers loose.

Check round.

And here's another smelly.

 NUMBER 37.

Not as good as the 34. Should have hooked that one when I had the chance. But never mind. 37'll trim up the journey a bit. Long as it's safe. And long as I can get to the stop quick. Run down the street. Panting now, bung-tired. Might not make it.

Glance back. Smelly's caught behind a van. That's cute. I needed a break. Run on, reach the stop, and here's the bus rumbling in. Step back, hood flopped over my face.

Eyeshine over the passengers. Not so many nebs on this one and they look like muffins. I'm going for it anyway. Doors open, nobody gets off. Jump on. Surly gobbo behind the wheel. Snag the ticket, find a seat, face low. Doors close. Smelly rolls off.

Check round again, slow, careful. Nobody looks dangerous. They just look tired. Like I must look tired.

Wonder what else they see. More than just a tired kid? A scared kid? A terrified kid?

Maybe they don't see anything. Maybe they're not even looking. Can't see any of 'em checking me out. Maybe that's how it is now, Bigeyes. I'm just nobody. Nobody worth bothering about. The only nebs who want me want me dead.

The rest of the world doesn't give two bells.

Smelly judders on down the road. Left at the end, judder, judder, on to the next stop, pull over. Like my life, Bigeyes. Judder, stop, judder, stop. Doors open. Feel my eyes whip round. Force of habit. They just do that. Don't have to think about it. Little queue of nebs crashing on.

Muffins.

Pretty sure.

Dip my head, let the hood fall lower. Nice and dark. Only it doesn't feel nice. Doesn't feel anything. It's just dark. Hear the doors close, then it's judder again, judder bloody judder.

I meant what I said, Bigeyes. I'm nothing now. Just a creature hiding in the dark, carried from one place to the next.

'Can you move up, please?'

Woman's voice. Sounds like an old dunny. Speaks again.

'You're half over the other seat and I can't sit down.'

I snick a glance up at her. Yeah, I was right. It is a dunny. Ancient too. Got hair sprouting round her mouth. Looks gross. I check her eyes, look for some snap. But they're soft, kind, bit like Mary's. She motions to the place next to me.

'I want to sit down and you're blocking the seat.'

I grunt, give her room.

'Thank you,' she says.

Sits down, settles herself. I dip my head, let the hood close over my face again. Hope she's not going to talk. Smelly rattles off. Dunny's quiet, just sitting there. But something's wrong. I can feel her body moving. It's up against mine. And it's trembling. Don't know why.

Then I feel it.

Again.

My hands on the knives. I got 'em stuffed under my coat and I'm gripping both hilts. Tight like before. Jesus, Bigeyes. When did I do that? Eh? I don't remember reaching under my coat. Don't remember taking 'em. And why? It's an old dunny, for Christ's sake. Who's she going to hurt?

She's still trembling. I can feel her old body shivering against me. I twist my head, sneak a look. Catch her staring at me, eyes wide. Maybe she's ill, got some medical condition. No, it's not that. Not with those eyes. She's choked out. And it's cos of me. I know it.

'Don't hurt me,' she murmurs.

She looks down at my coat, checks round like she's trying to attract attention. But nobody's watching. Looks quickly back at me.

'Don't hurt me.' She's pleading, low voice. 'I know you've

got something under your coat. A knife probably. I can't see what it is but I felt you reach for it. You're still holding it. I can tell. I'll give you my purse. Just don't hurt me.'

'I'm not going to hurt you.' I stare at her. 'And I don't want your money.'

She doesn't believe me. Look at her face, Bigeyes. Bungs another glance round. Still nothing from the other passengers. Nobody's noticed yet but they will soon. They'll clap she's not right. And they'll fix me straight. I got to stop her before she calls for help.

'I haven't got a knife, OK?'

I let go of the blades, pull my hands out, show 'em.

'See?'

She stares at 'em, looks up at my face. Still not sure.

I shrug.

'And I don't want your money.'

I give a huff, turn away, stare out the window. Just praying she keeps quiet. I don't need trouble from a dunny. Feel her stand up, edge away. Glance round. She's heading for the back of the smelly. Finds a seat, sits down, sees me watching, looks away.

I do the same.

Feel a shudder of pain.

Drop my head, pull the hood right over. Tears start again. I grit my jaw, breathe hard. Bastard tears. Got to stop 'em. I screw my eyes up, scowl into the dark. Hold 'em in somehow. But I'm wailing inside. Like Jaz that time I freaked her in the old hulk. When my face scared her so bad. And now I've freaked an old dunny. And I didn't mean to.

Can't take any more of this. Stand up, hood still low, walk to the door of the bus, hold on to the rail. Not looking back at the dunny. Not looking at anyone. But I can feel her watching. And the other nebs. All my instincts tell me they're watching.

All the nebs on the bus.

Maybe I'm wrong. My instincts aren't what they were. Don't know why. I've lost something. Since Mary and Jaz. Since Becky even. Far back as then. Since the day I found I couldn't kill any more.

Maybe no one's watching.

Not even the dunny.

And I'm just freaking my head for nothing. Cos I've lost it, Bigeyes, lost everything. I'm staring at the bonnet of the bus. Pull over, you bastard. I got to blast out of here. But the stop's another quarter of a mile.

I can still feel the wailing. It's deep inside me, like someone's screaming to get out of me. And I know who it is, Bigeyes. It's me. Screaming to get out of who I am. But I can't. I'm locked inside myself, like I'm locked inside this effing bus.

Change in the sound of the engine. Driver's crunching down the gears. Slowing down, bus stop pulling close. Nobody waiting. I glance round, check the faces. Looking down or away. None of 'em watching me. Not even the dunny.

She's talking to an old gobbo in the next seat.

Feel the smelly come to a halt.

Doors open. I stumble off, down the street, not looking back. Hear the doors close, engine rev. Moment later the smelly rolls past. I turn my head away. Don't want to see the dunny watching me. Wait till the bus has grumbled round the next bend, fix the street again.

Lots of nebs trigging up and down. Muffins, far as I can tell. Taxis, motors, bikes, more smellies. Cut down the next street, right at the end, through the playground, down the alley, out into New Cross Road.

And now we got to watch, Bigeyes.

Not just for grinks but for porkers. Cos this is where Hawk's dregs dropped off Jaz. Big building over there. See it? Halfway down on the right. And there's something they'll know. All of 'em. Porkers and grinks.

They'll know I won't keep away.

Cos of Jaz.

They'll know I'll be drawn to this place.

Like I am.

Don't suppose I'll get a glimpse of her. But I can't help myself. She's in there somewhere, Bigeyes. That big dronky building. They won't have taken her out yet. I'm sure of it. She'll be sitting in there. With Bannerman and Fern, I hope, or some decent porker.

I just hope she's OK.

I can't bear to think about what's happened to her.

I got pictures in my head, Bigeyes. I know the rooms in that place. Been in there myself enough times, specially up to the age of seven. That business I told you about with Bannerman and Fern, remember? The pedestrian crossing when I was seven?

In that building. That's where I was. And I've been in lots of the other rooms.

So where is she? My beautiful Jaz.

Down the street, keep behind the parked cars. Edge closer to the entrance. Check it out, Bigeyes. Steps up to the door. That's where they'll have dropped her. Bottom of those steps. Then crashed off in their motor.

She'll have stood right there. On that spot. Or maybe sat there.

Was she crying? Do you reckon she was crying? What state was she in? And here's another thing, Bigeyes. I didn't tell you this before, but I'm worrying about something else. What if Fern was zipping me over? She said Jaz is alive. But how do I know she was telling the truth?

It might have been a trick.

To get me to come in. Thinking I'd get to see Jaz. When she was never even there. That's what haunts me, Bigeyes. The thought that she might even be dead. Spite of what Fern said.

Nebs coming out the door. Pull back, crouch, check over the road, cute as I can. Two porkers in uniform, gobbo and a woman. Don't know 'em. Third neb. And I recognize her straight up. But it's not Jaz.

It's Bex.

26

SHE'S GOT HER head bowed and she's sloping down the steps. Looks choked out of her brain. I'm watching good, checking hard. Woman's got a hand hooked round Bex's arm, but not clamped. Looks almost motherly.

Making no difference.

Bex is freaked.

And I'm suddenly remembering something, Bigeyes. Think back, right? First time I rubbed shadows with her and we had a proper talk. After we wigged it out of the bungalow. She said something about the porkers, remember?

About being scared of 'em.

Not wanting to meet 'em, cos they'd send her back.

That's the word she used.

Back.

Only where's back? I'm starting to guess, Bigeyes. And it's cos of something else she said, another time, something about her dad. What he used to do to her on his boat. Are you cracking this? Eh? Cos I am. I'm seeing it clear. I got no proof and I could be wrong.

But I'm not.

OK?

I'm not.

Cos there's a third thing I remembered. Just now. Bex's name. All of it, I mean. Funny how I never thought about it before. Never clicked it in my head. But it's banging away now, like a mad screaming voice. That name, that bloody name.

Rebecca Jakes.

Jakes, Jakes, Jakes.

There's a porker called Jakes. Big dronk, high up in the police force. And he lives in the Beast. Another district, not close to here. I used to do jobs round his patch. Never brushed his stump. Kept clear of the bastard.

And he was a bastard. All the bums said so.

If he's Bex's dad, no wonder she looks bad.

Police motor drawing up. They're getting in. Gobbo bends down, opens the door, nods Bex in the back. Courteous, old-fashioned even. Woman's climbing in after her. Gobbo lumbers round the other side, climbs in too. Three in the back, Bex in the middle.

Yeah, yeah.

The porkers are being nice.

And careful too.

She might be freaked, but they're watching her cute. And now I'm getting the other thing. Clear as the pounding of my heart. The porkers didn't find her. She just gave herself up. Don't ask me how I know. And she's given up more than just herself.

She's given everything up.

Hope, caring, the whole stack.

I can guess what happened. She walked out of Ruby's place and up to the nearest porker. Or came straight to the station. Said here I am. I'm done. Finished. Jaz is gone and I've had enough. I got nowhere to go, nothing to care for. I know what's waiting for me.

The law.

And my dad.

But I don't care.

Car passes and she's gone. Christ, I feel bad. But I got to move on. Got to push Bex out of my head, got to act as if Jaz is really alive, and move on.

Back down the road, left at the end, left again, down to the crossroads, over to the park, through it and out the other side, down the steps to the bus stop. Wait, hood over my face. Smelly rolls in. Number 14.

Check the passengers, jump on, ticket from the driver.

Smelly rumbles off.

Two stops, three, four, checking faces. They're like bubbles in the sea. Floating on, floating off, too many to count. But I count 'em. I check 'em all.

Fifth stop, sixth stop.

Seventh, eighth, ninth.

Off the bus, left past the café, through the alleyway, out into the estate. Stop, under the walkway. Check round.

Check again.

Block of flats. Dronky brickwork, peeling window-frames. Kids kicking a football against the garage door further down. Gobbo bellows at 'em from inside the bottom-floor flat. They kick the ball one more time and wig it, laughing.

Silence.

I reach inside my coat, feel for the knives.

Slip round the building, in the back entrance, up to the first floor, wait. Still quiet. Up to the next floor, and the next, and the next. Not taking the lift. Too risky. Too easy to get boxed in.

One floor to go.

Still no sounds. It's like this place belongs to ghosts. Top floor. Down towards the end. Flat 22. Same colour door. Same stain on the outside. Same lock even. He might have moved. But I don't think so. Too lazy to shift his stump.

Ear to the door, listen. Usually got the television on when he's in. Or the radio. Or both. Even if he's got a woman. Which he usually has. Don't ask me what they all think. But they got to stack it or wig it. Cos the dungpot won't live without noise.

What did I tell you? Hear that?

Television on. Some game show. And another sound. Fainter, but you can clap it if you listen good. Hear it? Don't tell me I got to explain what it is. Try the door, soft.

Locked.

Down to Flat 23.

Stop, listen. No sound from inside. Listen again. Ring the bell, step back into the shadow, wait, watching both doors. Nothing. Just the sound of the television from Flat 22. And the other sound.

Back to Flat 23, whip out the knives. Lock picks easy. Open the door, snick in, close it behind me. Listen, feel, watch. No one here. I'm sure of it. But I got to check. Kitchen, loo, bedroom, lounge.

Dronky place.

Nobody here.

Pick up a chair, carry it over to the balcony door, step out. No sign of anyone watching from below. Take a breath, lift the chair, ease it over the rail onto next door's balcony, climb after it.

Squeeze the knives. One in each hand.

Peer through the door into Flat 22.

Nobody in the lounge. Just beer cans on the sofa and clothes on the floor outside the bedroom. Pick up the chair, stand back, fling it at the balcony door.

Glass shatters like a scream.

27

FROM INSIDE THE flat comes a bellow, but I'm already through. I'm into the lounge and racing for the bedroom. Door opens and there's his face peering out. Startled, scared, but still dangerous. Twenty-one years old and he's muscled out since I last saw him.

'Jesus!' he mutters.

Sees the blades coming for his eyes and jerks back. I prick his chest, nudge him back into the bedroom.

'Good boy, Ezi.'

He's naked but I got to watch him every second. His body's rippling and he's ready for a fight. He'll have a knife somewhere in here, maybe a gun. He'll be looking for a chance to snap it. His eyes flick over to the cabinet.

OK, it's in there. Gun probably. Got a feeling it's a gun. Prod him back onto the bed.

Black girl cowering in the corner. About fifteen. Starko

like him. Clutching a pillow to her chest. I give her a nod.

'You might want to go.'

She looks at Ezi. He takes no notice. He's got his eyes on me.

I ease him onto his back, one knife on his throat, the other on his jack. He's breathing hard but he's fixing me, trying not to show he's choked. The girl hasn't moved. I stab some more words at her.

'Get your clothes on and piss off!'

She scuttles round the bed. I check her quick, just a glance, then back. Can't take my eyes off Ezi for long. But she's a muffin, no sweat, breathing hard as she fumbles on her kit. I call out to her.

'And don't bother looking for Spit, sweetheart. Or anybody else. Time they get here, I'm gone.'

I lean closer to Ezi.

'And this guy's dead.'

Sound of running, front door opening, closing.

More running.

Down the corridor, down the stairs.

Silence.

Just me and Ezi. Him looking up, me looking down. He speaks, low voice.

'You know what I regret?'

I don't give him an answer. He's not waiting for one.

'Cutting up your back,' he goes on, 'and then letting you get away. Before we could rip up your front as well.'

He croaks out a laugh.

'But maybe there's still time.'

'I don't think so, Ezi.'

I fret the blades, just a bit, so he feels 'em. He stiffens.

'So what's this?' he breathes. 'Payback?'

'Kind of.' I fret the blades again. 'Only not for you.'

'Meaning?'

'I got bigger fish than you. And you got bigger fish than me.'

I watch him for a moment, then jump back off him. He stares up at me, not moving. I watch him for a moment, then whip back the knives. He flinches, half-curls up. I reach out, hold the blades over him. Then drop 'em on the bed beside him.

Step back.

Wait.

He straightens, sits up. Got his eyes hot on my face. I know what's coming and it happens quick. He snacks the blades, jumps up, rams his arm into my chest, pounds me back against the wall, knives nicking my throat. His voice comes rasping over me.

'Do it!' he roars. 'Do it, you shit!'

'Got no weapon, Ezi.'

'You must have. Knife, gun, whatever. Something in your coat.'

I shake my head.

'Only weapons I got, you got. In your clammy little hands.'

His face darkens. He shoves his bulk closer, squeezes it against me. He's still angry, still confused. And he doesn't believe me about the weapons.

'I told you,' I murmur. 'I got bigger fish than you. And you got bigger fish than me.'

'Like who?'

'Like the bastards scumming your people. And the big man at the top.'

'We already know them guys.'

'You don't know half of 'em. And you don't know the nob pulling their strings either. I reckon Nelson would be quite interested to know a bit about that. In fact, he'd be dead grateful to you for telling him. So would some of your other brethren. Like Fitz. Or Jimmy-Joe Spice.'

'They ain't brethren.'

'They will be. When they find out the same bums are scumming them too.'

More footsteps on the stairs, pounding close. Didn't take long. I knew the girl would shunt me. Door crashes open and here's the grit. Same age as Ezi but twice the size. I give him a wink.

'How you doing, Spit? Took your time getting here, didn't you?'

He stops, takes everything in, snarls at Ezi.

'Gimme them knives.'

Ezi's watching, still unsure. Spit doesn't wait. Beefs over, makes a grab for the blades. Ezi shifts, keeping 'em back. Spit glares at him, pulls out his own knife, lunges at me.

I let it come. Got to play this right. Split-second to stay, split-second to dodge. Got to let Ezi make his choice. If he will. He does, just in time. Reaches out, grabs Spit's wrist, checks the thrust. Knife's an inch from my heart.

Spit growls at him.

'Let go, man. I got to finish this shit.'

Ezi holds on.

'Not yet. Plenty of time, yeah?'

Spit stares at him for a moment, then at me. And smiles.

'Sure,' he drawls. 'Plenty of time. No rush.'

Yeah, Bigeyes. I know what's ticking his brain. And I'll tell you something else. I remember that smile. He had it when the two of 'em cut up my back. I saw it when I was facing 'em. And when they spun me over onto my front, and stuffed my face in the mud, and set to work with their blades, I still felt it.

The smile.

Leering down at me.

Even as I screamed.

I force a smile back.

'Trim me up again, Spitty, and you're dead. Want to know why? Cos too many people know about you. I made sure of that. I'm not stupid, OK? I left details. About you and Ezi. And all your little activities. Only reason you're not lemon peel is cos I said you could be useful. So watch your step. And you might just live.'

Spit doesn't answer. But he moves closer. I narrow my eyes.

'I could have taken Ezi out just now.'

'Why didn't you?' says Ezi.

'Yeah, why didn't I?' I fix Ezi again. 'Interesting question. So get this jerk out of my space and we'll talk.'

'You said you was after bigger fish.'

'I said get this jerk out of my space and we'll talk.'

I wait, keep my eyes on Ezi. Feel Spit take a step back. I glance over, look him up and down. Knife's still tight in his grip. I hold out a hand to Ezi.

'I'll have my two back.'

'You reckon.'

'Yeah, I do reckon. You don't need 'em. You got a gun in that drawer.'

Ezi looks over his shoulder at the cabinet, turns back.

'How did you know that?'

Jesus, Bigeyes. Some dronks are piss-thick.

'Never mind,' I say. 'Give me the knives. Go get your gun if it makes you feel safer.'

He doesn't move. But he gives me back the knives. I feel Spit brace himself. Give him a smile, stick the knives back inside my coat.

'OK, boys. Let's deal.'

28

THEY STAND BACK, but just a bit. Spit's staying between me and the door. He wants to kill me so bad. And rip me over first. Ezi's still mad too. They're holding back, both of 'em, cos they think I might have something. And they're worried I might not be bluffing about putting their names round, having nebs who'll come looking for 'em.

But they're still seething.

I got to act cool and talk chuck.

'OK, turn the television off.'

'What for?' says Ezi.

'Cos it's making a bloody row.'

'I like it on.'

'Turn it off.'

He fixes me, glances at Spit, back at me.

'We're wasting time,' I say. 'Turn the thing off.'

Ezi doesn't move. Spit grunts, then bustles off into the

lounge. I follow him out of the bedroom, Ezi close behind. Spit turns off the television, straightens up, sees the broken glass on the carpet.

'What happened to the balcony door?'

'Our little friend,' says Ezi.

I think of the money in my pocket. More than I should be carrying into a hole like this. I got to play things right and I got to act quick. Ezi's angry already and I don't want him worked up even more about the balcony door. But slipping him jippy won't help. It'll just make him dig into me for what I'm carrying.

Got to move this on fast.

'Yeah, sorry,' I mutter. 'Couldn't think of a better way in.'

I look quickly round the room.

'I need some paper and a pen.'

'Is this a joke?' says Spit.

Yeah right, Bigeyes. Can't imagine these slugs writing, can you?

'Paper and a pen,' I tell him. 'Got to write some stuff down.'

'Just tell us what it is,' says Ezi.

'You won't remember.'

'Try us.'

They're moving closer again. They don't believe me. I got to watch my step or everything'll split.

'I got names you want,' I say. 'Big names. Names Nelson's going to want to know about.'

'We can remember names,' Spit mutters.

'Not this many. And it's not just names. It's places where you'll find 'em. And more. Stuff you won't remember. I need paper and a pen. Wait here.'

I head for the balcony door.

Spit steps in front of me, blocking the way.

'Where you going?'

'Next door had a telephone pad. I saw it when I came through.'

'I'll get it.'

His eyes punch into mine.

'You don't move.'

He glances at Ezi, lumbers out onto the balcony, climbs over to next door, disappears. Back again a few moments later, pad and pen in one hand, knife in the other. Clambers back into the flat.

Ezi's still standing close. Hasn't gone to fetch his gun, but he's pulled on some trousers and he's watching me cute. Spit hands me the pad and pen. I take it, start writing. Feel 'em move close again, one either side. I look up, check 'em over, look down again.

Write on.

'Now listen,' I murmur, still writing. 'You don't get this for nothing.'

Stop writing. Check 'em over again.

They're closer still.

Watching.

I tear off the first piece of paper.

'Which one of you can read?'

'Bastard,' growls Spit.

Ezi takes the paper, runs his eye down it.

'Don't know these names.'

'You don't, do you?' I lean closer. 'But they know you. And Spitty. And all the creepy-crawlies you hang out with. And not only that. They know the rest of your joint. All the way up to Mr Nelson. And they know all about his activities.'

I hold out my hand.

'Give me back the paper.'

Ezi hands it to me. I crumple it up in my fist, throw it over my shoulder onto the floor. Both of 'em stiffen.

'What you do that for?' mutters Ezi.

'Cos you don't need 'em. They're small fry. They're creepy-crawlies too. You can forget about them.'

He won't, Bigeyes. And I don't want him to.

I want Nelson's shades to sort every dronk on that list.

But that's no bum gripe. Ezi'll pick up the list later.

I start writing again. Spit and Ezi close in like before, but not for the same reason. They're craning over my shoulder, reading the names. And now they're interested. You better believe it.

'I know them names,' Spit says.

Course he does. They both do. Every name on the list is a big nob in their world. Small fry in Hawk's world. Just spear-carriers for Hawk. Cos that's what these dronks don't get. To them, Nelson's the top man.

And he's big in his own little pond.

Like Fitz and Spice.

And all the others.

Yeah, there's lots of 'em. Big in their own little ponds.

But Hawk creams the lot. And they never know. Cos they don't even know he exists. All they know is who they meet. The grinks who carry out his work. Some of 'em on that list on the floor. And now, on this other list, a few of the ones higher up.

The spikes.

Not the ones near the top. Nelson's muck doesn't deal with them, doesn't know about them. But these names . . .

I hand Ezi the list. He reads it, holds it out to Spit.

'We know these guys,' he says.

I shake my head.

'No, you don't. You just think you do.'

'We work with 'em.'

'They're scumming you. And they're scumming Nelson. And every bum joint you work with.'

Silence.

Sound of footsteps outside in the corridor, women's voices, low.

Silence again.

'This don't mean nothing,' says Spit. 'It ain't no proof or whatever.'

I tear off several sheets of paper, step back, sit down at the table.

'Now what you doing?' says Ezi.

'This'll take a bit longer. So I'm sitting down.'

They don't move, but I feel 'em watching close. I start writing, slow, careful. Got to get everything right. This all happened over three years ago. Just as well I remember so good. It comes flooding back. Dates, places, everything, like the pen's doing the talking by itself.

Feels funny to be writing.

Even simple stuff.

Never done much writing. Never needed to. Like I told you, I never went to school. But here's something, Bigeyes. Chew on this. Know who taught me to read and write?

You guessed it.

Hawk.

And here I am, writing words to bring him down. Not that these words will. He's too powerful for anything I can do here. But they'll help. They'll start the fire. Look at 'em, Bigeyes. Tiny little words.

Falling like sparks.

All the scams, all the stings.

Nothing the porkers can use. This is scum against scum. And it won't reach up to the top. But like I say, it'll start the fire. And Hawk'll feel some of the heat.

I stop writing, hold up what I got. Several sheets.

Ezi and Spit come close again, slow.

And I can feel the change in 'em. Yeah, Bigeyes, see the difference? They're thinking, let him write it all out, give us what we want. Then take him out.

I shake my head.

'Taking me out won't help you one bit. Cos I'm not giving you all the information here. Read that. Go on. Read it.'

Ezi takes the sheets, starts to read. Spit doesn't. He's watching me.

Eyes hard.

'It's all there,' I murmur. 'Everything you want. Every scam, every little trick. Every enemy you got and never knew you had. How do I know all that? Cos I was part of it. You hate me cos I took out some of your tribe. But I'm nothing in all this, just like you're nothing. Nelson's been stitched a hundred times and he doesn't even know it. And the scumbos on that list are the ones responsible. The ones he thought were his friends.'

Ezi goes on reading.

Spit goes on watching.

Comes over. Stands by the table, looking down.

I stare up at him, then past at his mate. Ezi finishes reading, comes over. Looks down too. And it's still there, Bigeyes. In their faces. What they want. I speak, slow, clear.

'So here's the deal.'

They don't answer. Just watch. Ezi's clutching the paper tight. His other hand's squeezing into a fist. I think of the knives in my coat. Don't want to use 'em. I need these dronks alive. Killing dregs won't touch Hawk, won't even brush his brain.

'So here's the deal,' I go. 'You got this information. Nelson's going to want it. So are Fitz and Spice and all the others. Cos it affects them too. Now listen. Nelson's getting all this from me. And in return . . .'

'Yeah?' says Ezi.

I pause, hold their eyes.

'In return . . . Nelson, Fitz, and Spice keep their people off my back.'

'Deal,' says Ezi.

It won't be, Bigeyes. Course it won't. Gangster bosses like Nelson and the other two would never honour such a deal. They'll take the information I've given 'em and still want me dead. I've turned over too many of their dronks to make 'em like me. But that's cute. I wasn't looking for protection. Not really. Just pretending I was. I want 'em to have the information. So they can use it.

And that's it.

And they got to have it this way. They wouldn't take it otherwise, wouldn't trust it, not even from your normal grass and certainly not from me if I just offered it without wanting something back. But give 'em a deal to slap down and they're sweet as pie. But that's just the easy bit done.

Now's the hard part.

Getting out of here.

I stand up.

'There's four more names,' I say. 'The big ones. I'll phone 'em through to you in half an hour.'

'Give 'em now,' says Spit.

I square up to 'em. They're standing firm, blocking my way.

I think of the knives again, feel 'em inside my coat, hard against my sides. I narrow my eyes, lower my voice.

'Kill me and you don't get the juice.'

They don't speak. I go on, slow.

'You got most of the goods. Plenty to get on with. But not the big stuff. The really big stuff. The top four names. I'll give you those when I'm safe out of here.'

Spit's face darkens. I whisper at him.

'Yeah, big guy, you want to screw 'em out of me so bad, don't you? And you know what? You might even manage it. But think for a moment. What if I don't talk? Cos I just might not. And then what? Cos remember what I said. There's bigger fish for all of us. Much much bigger. So ask yourself the question. What's Nelson going to say when you lose the top guys just for the pleasure of dicking me?'

I pause.

'Specially when you know that if Nelson doesn't plug you, my friends will. When they catch up with you later.'

Spit's jaw twitches, falls still. I glance at Ezi.

'What's your mobile number?'

He doesn't answer.

'Ezi.'

'What.'

'What's your mobile number?'

He shrugs.

'I'll write it down.'

'Don't bother. Just tell me.'

'But—'

'Just tell me. I remember numbers.'

Spit's jaw twitches again. Ezi mumbles the number, like he doesn't want me to hear. But I catch it, stick it in my head.

'Step aside,' I say.

They don't. They just watch me, hard, angry.

'Step aside,' I snarl.

They go on watching. Then slowly step aside.

I walk between 'em, over to the door of the flat, open it, look back.

Slip away.

29

DOWN THE CORRIDOR, down the steps, fast as I can, soft as I can. Got to wig it quick, but not so they hear me blasting out. No time to spill though. They'll be having second thoughts, maybe ringing round right now to clan up.

Place could be surrounded before I hit the ground floor.

But there's nobody.

Not yet. Just a couple of trolls slumped by the door. Sound of voices outside, but it's kids. I stop, take a breath, push out into the courtyard. Three boys chipping up at me. Look about eleven.

'What you staring at?' says one.

I don't stop. There's danger round here. Too much, too close. I can feel it. Boy blags off at me again.

'Wanker!' he jeers.

Gives me the finger, giggles to his mates.

Jesus, Bigeyes. I want to whip out the knives, nick his ears. Does he know how many nebs I'd killed by the time I was his age? Obviously not, cos he's still smirking at me.

Shadow over to the right, behind the bins.

Another further back. And I'm sensing more.

Might be nothing to do with Ezi and Spit. There's gangs and gangs round here. But I'm not waiting to find out. Out of the gate, over the street, through the estate.

Checking round, cute as I can. I'm not worried about the younger dronks. It's the big boys I'm bombed about. We're not talking about teen gangs, Bigeyes. We're talking about what teen gangs want to grow into.

There's bad shit out there. Nelson's got some of it working for him. And he's not the only gangster bojo. Fitz and Spice you've heard of, but there's more. And here's something.

Not one of 'em's heard of Lord Haffler-Devereaux.

You cracking this?

Not one of 'em.

If anyone's heard of him, it's as a public benefactor. Nothing to do with their pimping and pushing. They'll know some of his spikes. The bastards they thought were allies, the ones I've just blotched on. But they won't know who's at the top.

Playing 'em to death just for fun.

And they're not the only nebs who don't know about Lord H.

Society doesn't know either. Some nebs will have heard of him—aristos mostly, or political toffs, or business

bums—but only as a saint. Someone the world can trust.
I mean, you couldn't give that much money to charity
and not be a saint, now could you?

I'll tell you something, Bigeyes.

If there's genius in evil, he's got it.

Cos here's what's clever: you got all these gangster
pods ripping round the Beast, each with its own bojo in
charge. And they're all the same. The bojos, I mean.
Jumped-up little dictators who think they're big shots cos
they've creamed some frosty money and haven't got
caught yet.

And cos they got zip loads of trash like Ezi and Spit to
screw stumps if anyone gets in the way. Yeah, they're all
the same. But here's the thing: you got all these bojos and
their joints scrapping on the same patch, and all that
jippy coming in from drugs and sex and all the other shit,
but somehow nobody's noticed that the money they're
raking in all ends up trickling to the same place.

Hawk's nest.

That's right. The jippy ends up in the hands of a man
they don't even know they're working for and haven't
even heard of. And what does he use it for? Not drugs,
that's for sure. Or sex. Or anything the bojos and their
crushers fight over. No, he's got a much higher
purpose.

Terror.

That's right.

And why? I told you already.

The Game.

That's what the money's for. That's what the terror's for.

Wrecking.

Economies, businesses, lives, whatever. It's about waiting, hitting, moving in, taking over. This is a war, Bigeyes. Might not look like one but it is. For Hawk and his fellow slime.

I don't know what they want. Not in detail. Could be anything. But I told you before, it's global. And it's about change. And that means destruction on a massive scale. That's why they're hitting finance. Creating instability. Supporting factions around the world. Whatever's needed.

And there's one thing they really like.

Oh yeah. Yummy yummy.

Arms.

What kind of arms? How high do you want to go? All the way to the top? OK, let's go there. Cos that's how high Hawk wants to go. As high as it gets. So Christ knows who the slimeheads are talking to. All I know is, sooner or later, someone's going to sell 'em what they want.

And then you'll know it's a war.

End of the estate, past the shop, round the corner. Smelly bumping down. Number 17. Check the passengers, jump on, seven stops, off again. Over the road, through the cemetery, into the park.

Stop by the monument.

Check round.

Looks safe. Young mum with a pram. Ancient gobbo on

the bench, smoking a roll-up. Couple of dog walkers. Check again, cute as I can. Pull out the mobiles I got left. Not working.

Half-expected it. Drop 'em on the ground, back of the monument, out the gate, down the street to the super-market. Check faces, in through the door. Might as well make it two birds with one stone while we're here.

And Christ, I'm hungry.

Sandwiches, apples, sausage rolls, bottle of mineral water. Back for more sausage rolls. Checkout. Girl's look-ing me over, quizzical. But she keeps quiet. Hand her a note, snap the change, out of the supermarket, over to the payphone across the street.

One coin'll do. Cos I'm not saying much.

Dial, wait. Voice grunts into my ear.

'Yeah?'

Ezi's not big on social skills.

'Got something to write with?' I say.

'No. We lost the pen and paper.'

'Well, find something.'

Sound of muttering. I check the street. Two gobbos walking towards the supermarket. Suits. Might be muf-fins, might be grinks. Hard to tell. Not looking my way. But I don't like the smell of 'em. Ezi comes back.

'I got a pencil.'

'Got some paper or something?'

'I can write on the wall.'

I'm still watching the gobbos. They've stopped. One of 'em's fixing me from the other side of the road. Other's pulled out a mobile. Check round. If they're grinks, there'll be more close by or these two would be over by now.

But there's nobody. Nobody I can see anyway.

'Write this down,' I mutter. 'Lord Haffler-Devereaux.'

'Eh?' says Ezi.

I spell the name for him.

'Who the hell's Lord Haffler-Devereaux?' says Ezi.

'The biggest name on your list. Tell Nelson. Tell everybody. You got no bigger enemy than him. I got to go now.'

'But where's the bastard hang out?'

'Look him up. You'll find him easy. I got to go.'

The gobbos are moving across the street. Heading straight here. Ezi moans at me.

'What about the other names? You said there was four.'

'I was lying. There's only one. But he's enough.'

I kill the phone, step out. Gobbos have spread apart. No question who they are now. But these two aren't the danger. That's going to come from somewhere else.

Don't ask me how I know.

Got it.

Other end of the street.

Two more, closing in.

30

BACK INTO THE supermarket, past the checkouts, down the first aisle. Glance round. Two of the gobbos crunching after me. Step round the shoppers. Old dunny in the way, pushing her trolley.

'Mind out!' she splutters.

Jig round her, on towards the far end of the store.

Emergency exit.

Bang through, outside. Collection depot. Couple of vans, two drivers leaning out the windows, naffing. Check round. Gobbos barging on, one muttering into his phone.

Round the corner, back towards the street. Still clutching the bag of food. Sound of footsteps behind, slamming on the pavement. I got a head start but it's not much, and the other two'll show any moment.

Unless I get to the street first.

I do, just.

But the grinks are close behind. And here's their mates,

belting in from the right. Down the street, back the way I came. If I can just get to where I was aiming, I'll be safe for a bit. But only if I throw 'em off.

Least they can't do much with these shoppers around.

But it won't last. And there'll be more dregs crowding in now these ones have clapped me. Check round. They've slowed down. Close behind but hanging back, trying to look normal, waiting for the moment. Two talking on mobiles.

I catch a smile from one.

A chilly smile.

Yeah, grink. You think you got me.

But not yet.

Cos here's something I want. Post van, door open, engine running. And nice Mr Postie over the road, handing a parcel to the gobbo in the bakery. Run down, bung the supermarket bag on the passenger seat with the letters, jump in, close the door, rev up.

Van shoots off.

Yeah, baby.

Scraggy motor. Sings like a crow. But who cares? Check the mirror. Grinks standing still, watching me go. They know they can't run. Not worth it, not here. But Postie's running. Look at him. Cracking his guts to keep up.

Sorry, mate.

You can have it back soon. I'm not going far.

He gives up, stops, looks round for help.

But now I'm gone. Down the street, left at the end, right at the lights, right again. I'm heading the wrong way, then cutting back the right way. Just to throw off the porkers when Postie tells 'em which way I went.

Don't think he got a glimpse of my face. But someone probably did. So the porkers'll be flooding the area too. Just as well I got a place to hide.

It's not a snug, Bigeyes. No snugs in the Beast. But it's where I was planning to slap it for the next few hours. Till it gets dark.

Past the multistorey car park, round the roundabout, over the lights, left at the pub, pull over. Check round. Dronky place, yeah? Who'd want to live here? Terrace houses but they're crumbling, see?

Anyway, come on. We got to move. Got to walk back.

But a different way.

Grab the supermarket bag, out of the van, check the street. Kids at the far end, three gobbos on the bench, looking the other way. Don't think they saw me get out of the van. Can't be worrying anyway. Start to walk off.

Stop.

Back to the van. Check the street again. Don't ask me why I'm doing this. I don't know. OK, I do. I'm cranked about Postie, all right? It's not his fault I creamed his motor. Well, it is. But I don't want him getting stuffed cos of me.

Losing his mail as well as his van.

Reach in, rip out the ignition key, lock the van. Bend down, drop the key on the ground, up against the inside of the front wheel. And now let's go.

Down the street, round the back of the industrial estate, over the main road, down the alleyway, out the other side. OK, see where we are? Look straight ahead. Recognize that?

The park where I tried to use the mobiles.

Only last time we came at it from the other side. Through the cemetery, remember? There's the monument where I dropped the phones. Wonder if someone's picked 'em up. But never mind that. We won't be checking. I got something else to show you.

Only we got to play stealth now.

And that's hard to do in daylight.

Round the edge of the park. Still quite a few nebs about. Muffins, far as I can tell. Woman walking a poodle, kid on a bike, elderly couple sitting on the bench. Walk on, hood up, face low. Seem to have lost that beanie I had.

Never mind.

We're not far now.

Edge of the park, move slow. Round to the side gate, past it, on to where the kiosk used to be, over the path, into the knot of trees. Check again. Main part of the park's over to the right now. You can still see the monument from here. Just the back. Got it?

Now look to the left.

Kind of a dip, then a few old slabs of stone.

Come with me. And keep low. Cos this is a funny place. Druggies hang around here. It's a shithole for a den but it does keep out the wind. And there's a secret even the needles don't know about.

I got shown it by a duff when I was nine. And he died a year later. So maybe no one else knows about it now. Or hardly anyone. Let's hope so anyway.

Down into the dip, stop, check round. Nobody here. Walk on, slow. Got to pick your way carefully. The slabs are all lumpy, see? And with the trees overhead, you're kind of hidden in a little nook.

Stop again.

Look around you, Bigeyes. This is where the druggies sit. You can see some of their wreckage on the stones. Now look again. Forget the crap. Tell me what else you see.

Yeah, yeah. I know what you're thinking. It's just slabs of stone on top of each other. Well, it's not. Far corner, check it out. There's a gap, see? You can squeeze through that. If you're small enough.

The druggies don't bother with it. Nor do the duffs. Too narrow. And nothing much in there—they think. But this other duff—the one I told you about—he was a skinny bastard. And he showed me what's really inside, if you know how to look.

It's not cute, Bigeyes. But I'll tell you what.

It's useful.

Come on.

Drop the supermarket bag in, squeeze through the gap, ease down, feel for the ledge. This is tough. I'm bigger than I was last time I wriggled in here, and I got pockets bulging too. But here's the ledge under my feet.

I'm in.

Sit down on the hard rock, breathe, wait.

Darkness, darkness.

Wait, keep waiting, let it settle. It does, slow. And now I'm seeing it again. The little closed space. Tiny gap above where we slipped in, chilly chamber below, where we are now. Dead rat in the corner. Cans and bottles and syringes that nebs have dropped through the gap over the years.

And that's it.

Only it's not. Cos there's more.

And this is what the old duff really wanted to show me. But to show you, Bigeyes, we got to crawl. Over there, far end, where the top of the rock pushes down. Going to be a scrape. So you better close your eyes if you freak out in confined spaces.

Slow, slow, nice and slow. Worth it to be safe. And right now there's few places we can call safe. Specially in the Beast with grinks and porkers spilling close. And they will be, Bigeyes. Trust me.

They'll be buzzing this area by now.

Only risk here is if they send dogs.

Let's just hope they don't.

End of the chamber, stop where the rock comes down. Now check it cute, Bigeyes. I know it's hard in the dark, but look it over good. It's not the wall, see? It's an overhang. It looks like it's the end of the wall but it's not. Cos the darkness distorts it.

The rock comes down almost to the level of the floor but there's another gap at the bottom. And you can squeeze under that too. If you do it right.

Push the supermarket bag ahead of me, breathe in, flat on the floor, pull myself under. Never liked this bit. And it was easier when I was smaller. But it's not just about size. It's about how you do it. Halfway through now, bit further, bit further, done. Pull myself out the other side.

And now look.

Another chamber. And a tunnel heading down.

Into the dark.

31

ON, ON, DOWN, down. Still cramped, but least it's hands and knees now, not flat on the floor. And it gets better soon. I could probably stay here and be OK, but I still don't feel safe. Not when there's somewhere much better just a short way on.

Two spots in the darkness. Two more.

Just rats.

They skitter up, nose round the bag. I shove 'em off. They disappear down the tunnel. Creep on. And here's the shaft. Tunnel goes a bit further, see? Where the rats just went. But we're climbing down here.

Check it out.

Know what this is? You should have worked it out by now. Well, I'm not telling you. You'll find out anyway in a minute. But we got to climb down first. Don't worry. It's easy piss. Check out those wooden ribs. Plenty of 'em to grab hold of.

And we're only talking about a little climb.

Half a minute and we're done.

OK, I was wrong.

Two minutes. But I haven't been here for a few years, all right? And I'm carrying a supermarket bag. Anyway, check around, Bigeyes.

Another tunnel, much bigger, see? Or higher anyway. Doesn't go very far. And we're not going exploring. No point. It's blocked both ends. But check out the shape of the walls. Worked it out now?

Jesus, Bigeyes. You just don't notice stuff.

Well, here's a clue. If I took you down that way for a couple of minutes, you'd find some rusty old tracks running along the ground. They don't join up with anything. They run out just before the tunnel gets blocked off at the other end.

Now you get it, right?

We're in one of the old snakeholes. There's loads of these tunnels under the Beast. Some of 'em have got track, some of 'em haven't. Don't know if any trains ever ran on 'em. Maybe they were just started and never finished.

Most of 'em aren't that secret.

So we can't use 'em.

But this one's a little beauty. And we'll slap it here for a bit.

While we wait for the evening. And what's coming next.

Slump on the ground, back against the wall. Breathe

slow, breathe again. Pull the supermarket bag over, dig about for the sausage rolls. More spots in the darkness. More squeakies.

Yeah, boys, you want some of this, don't you?

Well, you can't have it.

I kick out. Hear the rats scuttling away. Don't mind 'em much. Quite like 'em even. When you've dug around with as much scum as I have, rats are nothing. They can hang about here if they want. Long as they don't try and bog my food.

Gulp it down.

God, I'm hungry.

Gulp, gulp.

Squeakies come back, watch. I go on eating, bag clutched on my lap. Finish the sausage rolls, start on the sandwiches. Finish 'em, eat the apples, chuck the cores into the darkness. Drink the mineral water. Bung the bottle away.

Lean back.

Breathe again.

Rats have gone.

Pull out the money from all my pockets, check it over. Put a bit back. Enough to get by. No point carrying all the jippy. Too risky. Could lose the lot in one go. So I'll leave most of it here.

Should be safe enough. Long as the squeakies don't eat it.

Shove the bundle of notes in the supermarket bag, stand up, check the wall. Roll up the bag, wedge it high as I can in a gap in the rock, stand back. Good spot. You can't even see it in the darkness. Unless you're looking for it.

We'll take a chance.

Slump back on the ground.

And now I got to work.

Pull out the paper and pen. Didn't see me take this, did you? When I was with Ezi. That's cos you don't watch, Bigeyes. I told you before. OK, now listen. I got writing to do. Lots of it.

So keep out of my way.

I got to think.

And I got to remember.

Lots of gump.

Write, write, write. Never mind what it is. You'll find out later.

Some of it's what I gave Ezi and Spit. But only a bit.

Write, write.

Hands aching, eyes feel grainy. Scratch 'em, lean back. And there's the little spotty lights again. Just two this time. One squeaky friend. Looks at me. And I look back. Into the darkness

And you know what, Bigeyes?

Suddenly feels like I'm looking back into another darkness. Like it was in the old city. Shit, I miss her. She was a bitch sometimes, but I still miss her. And you know what I miss most from that place?

The little snug I showed you.

The one with all the books, remember? The one with

Treasure Island and that thing about Nietzsche. And *The Wind in the Willows*. The book I read that night. In the darkness. Cos that's my life, Bigeyes. Darkness.

I read in it. I write in it.

I live in it.

Like Ratty over there.

'Ratty,' I murmur.

And I'm thinking of *The Wind in the Willows* again, and Ratty and Mole, and that bit when Moley goes out and gets lost in the Wild Wood, and the snow comes down, and the voices start whispering all around him.

And he's scared.

Till Ratty comes and rescues him.

I look at the tiny eyes. They go on watching, then disappear. Look down again, write on, on, on, stop. Lean back, pull out the knives, rest 'em on my lap. Think of Becky, Mary, Jaz.

Try to calm down. But it's hard. I can feel my heart blamming away inside me. Squeeze the knives, stare round the dark space. And it's like time's never been, never existed. Cos there's something I didn't tell you, Bigeyes. Yeah, I know. Yet another thing.

I was slumped here three years ago.

Same spot.

Exactly.

And you know what day that was?

The day I left the Beast and ran away. Thinking I'd never come back. Knowing Becky was dead. And that it was my fault. I sat here, staring out, like I'm doing now.

Could be the same moment.

All over again.

Cos nothing's changed. Nothing at all.

Except more nebs have died.

I drop my head, squeeze the knives again. The blades glint in the darkness. I close my eyes, think of what I want. What I must have.

I'm desperate to get started. I want to go now, right now. But I can't. I know I can't. Got to make myself be patient, wait till evening, till it's good and dark up top. But I can't leave it too late either. There's too much to do.

So it's wait, wait, wait. Then move, watch.

And hit the place.

At just the right time.

32

ONLY IT'S THE wrong time.

Half seven, the clock says. The one on top of the television. I've been here fifty minutes and still nothing. Suppose I couldn't have known for sure. It was always going to be a guess. But a good guess though. Cos this crapper's a creature of habits.

One of 'em over there in the drinks cabinet.

Check round the room.

Never been in here before. But it's what I expected. A living room that's not lived in. One set of curtains drawn back, other set drawn across. Don't ask me what that means. All I know is it's dark and the heating's off and it's getting late.

Eight o'clock, quarter past.

Click of the front door.

I tense up. Hall light goes on. Stabs under the living room door. Feel my way along the wall. Cough on the other side of the door. Sound of post being slit open, dropped on the hall table. Footsteps heading this way.

I edge behind the door.

It opens and the shadow walks in. I slip up behind, whip both knives over the throat. The figure stiffens, holds still. We stand there, quivering against each other. He speaks, low voice.

'There's thirty people you could be.' He takes a slow breath. 'But only one I was expecting tonight.'

I sniff.

'There's more than thirty dronks want a piece of your face, Bannerman.'

'Lucky for me you're not one of them.'

'Sure about that?'

'I think so.'

'Want to find out?'

I move the blades up and down his throat.

'What do you want?' he mutters.

'I've come to deal.'

'Knives won't help you do that.'

'I think they will.'

He grunts.

'They'll only help you if you're prepared to use them. And I don't think you are any more.'

I rasp 'em over his skin, one either side, fix 'em on the carotid arteries. Feel him swallow. I lean closer, murmur into his ear.

'But you don't know for certain, do you, Pugface? You can't be sure. I mean, no one can. Even I can't. That's what's scary. Maybe I want to give up the knife but I got no power to stop myself. Cos it's part of me. Like you and your drinks cabinet.'

'It's empty.'

'No, it isn't.'

'Looked inside, have you?'

'Had to do something while I was waiting for you. And guess what. It's stocked up like you got a regiment coming to stay. Jesus, no wonder you never get promoted.'

Silence. Just the sound of traffic outside the house. And Bannerman's heavy breaths. I keep behind him, blades tight on his neck, check him over. He's staying still, looking straight ahead, watching his step.

He's smart. Trust me, Bigeyes. He might be an alco but he's brained up. Maybe he really was expecting me. I almost believe him. He speaks suddenly, new voice. Kind of conversational.

'Weirdest thing happened today.'

He pauses for a moment, like he's waiting for me to say something. But I don't.

'Boy called Damien,' he goes on. 'Rich kid, super rich. Daddy's got so much money he could practically buy the city. Anyway, Damien gets kidnapped outside his school and taken off in a car.'

I say nothing. Just keep the knives firm on Bannerman's neck. He chugs on, chatty like before.

'Witnesses gave us a fascinating description of the kidnapper. But here's what's strange. Damien gets driven off, then suddenly he turns up again, safe and sound, just an

hour or two later. All Daddy can tell us is someone anony-
mous rang and left a tip-off. And they found the boy in an
old garage.'

'What's your point, Bannerman?'

'Just that it's strange.' He pauses again. 'And here's
something even stranger. Damien got found just after little Jaz turned up at the police station. Like you told us
she would. So obviously, you know, I'm wondering.'

'Wondering what?'

'Whether you know something about Damien too.'

Yeah, Bigeyes, he wants to play games. Well, he's on his
own.

'Listen,' I start.

But he cuts in sharp.

'Ever heard of a guy called Pink?' His voice has changed
again. More kick. He doesn't wait for an answer. 'Harvey
Samuelson Pink. If you want his full name. Owns a chain
of casinos and other . . . establishments. Ever heard of
him?'

'Might have.'

'He got shot an hour ago.'

I stiffen.

'Coming out of a restaurant,' says Bannerman. 'Died
instantly. Big crowd with him. Minders, family, friends. It
was his daughter's birthday party, apparently. Two guys on
a motorbike. Drove up, three shots into Pink, gone. Nobody
else got hurt. So I guess it's pretty clear who they wanted.'

Christ, Bigeyes, it's started quicker than I thought. First
name on Ezi's list. Hard to know who cracked it. Nelson's

dronks probably. Pink will have been a personal slam for him. But Nelson won't do it all on his own. He'll be naffing with Fitz and Spice.

And the other bojos.

There's going to be blood, Bigeyes. Just wish it was Hawk's too. But it won't be. Not this way. They got his name, yeah, but he'll be too clever for all of 'em. Bringing Hawk down'll take more than two gobbos on a motorbike. Specially now he knows the bojos are on to him.

'So what's this deal?' says Bannerman.

No fear in his voice now. None at all. I still got the knives over his carotid arteries but he sounds almost relaxed. He's even stopped shaking. I got to choke him up a bit or I'll get nothing from him.

I flick the blades, fret 'em on the skin, squeeze a trickle of blood down the left side of his neck. Feel him stiffen again, feel his breathing pump up. Squeeze another trickle of blood, right side. Feel his body go tight.

Wait, watch.

Whisper.

'Now listen good, Pugface. I give you something. You give me something.'

'That's normally how deals work.'

'Don't get clever, Bannerman.'

'What in it for me?'

'Information.'

'What kind of information?'

'Big stuff. Bigger than you can believe.'

'Why give it to me?'

'Cos you're the only person who'll give me what I want.'

He twitches his hands. I don't see it, just feel it. They're loose by his sides but he's kept 'em still all this time. I fret the blades again, let him feel the edges, just a bit. His hands fall still. He takes a long breath, speaks again.

'What is it you want?'

'I want to see Jaz.'

His hands twitch again, fall still.

'Just once,' I say. 'And you know where she is. You got her somewhere safe. I know people are going to take her away soon. Foster parents, whoever. But I'm guessing they haven't taken her yet and I want to see her before she goes.'

'Maybe she's gone already,' says Bannerman.

He's lying, Bigeyes. He's zipping me over. Don't ask me how I know. Testing me to see if I choke.

Jesus, Bigeyes, tell me I'm right.

'She hasn't gone,' I growl. 'Not yet. She's still here. Someone's looking after her. Someone from the police. The foster people haven't come yet. Tomorrow maybe. But not yet.'

It's no good, Bigeyes. I can hear my voice trembling.

And Bannerman will have heard it too.

He waits, like he's playing with me. Then he speaks—and his voice has changed yet again. Like it's softer.

'She's been asking for you.'

I feel myself tense up.

'She's been calling out your name,' says Bannerman. 'Blade, Blade, Blade. Keeps calling for you. And the Jakes girl. Becky.'

'She's called Bex, not Becky.'

'Whatever. Jaz keeps calling for her too.'

'Is Bex with her?'

'No, she's . . . being reunited with her father and step-mother.' A pause. 'Her father's a senior police officer. But maybe you know that.'

I tense up again. I can't handle this, Bigeyes. Got thoughts and feelings flooding me. Can't get my head straight. Can't get anything straight. Got to focus on Jaz. She's what I came here for. And I got one chance to see her before they take her away.

Don't mind what happens after that. Long as she's happy. That's all that counts. Doesn't matter about me. But I want to see her, I got to see her, one more time.

I tighten the blades over Bannerman's throat.

'I want to see Jaz,' I breathe. 'Just me and her alone. And I want you to fix it. Right now. No tricks, no arrest, nice and simple. I see Jaz. You get your information. And I walk free. That's the deal. OK?'

Another silence. A long one.

Then he moves.

Fast.

I'm quick—Jesus, I'm quick—but he slams me like a scud. Before I can plug him, he's got both my wrists clamped in his hands, then the knives wrenched out, and now he's turned, holding 'em both, and he's facing me, eyes bright and fixed.

I take a step back, feel the wall behind me. Bannerman kicks the door shut, moves closer, stops. Leans down.

'Deal,' he murmurs.

Then hands me back the knives.

'Let's go,' he says.

33

WE DON'T TALK in the car. Not a word. I watch the streets slip by. Nebs crowding everywhere: bars, cafés, clubs, restaurants. Porkers spilling round. Grinks too, probably.

Only I don't see 'em.

Cos I don't care. I'm hardly watching. Not right now. Maybe they'll clap me, maybe they won't. Don't give two bells. I got one thing in my head. That's all.

I'm going to see Jaz.

I think.

Cos here's the thing. Bannerman could be lying. Might just be driving me to the police station. Taking a dronky route if he is, but that could be part of the rip. To sting me into thinking he's cool when he's not.

And I wouldn't blame him. Shunting me, I mean. I'd probably do the same if I was him. Multiple murderer, the kid everyone's looking for, and here he is blobbed in my car. I'd take the little shit straight in.

Only Bannerman's different. That's why I'm taking the risk. I mean, he might be an alco and a sad git, but he's a good porker. And he might just be an honest one.

I glance at him. Got his lips tight together.

'Struggling, aren't you, Pugface?'

'Over what?'

'Handing me in. Or not.'

'Not struggling over that,' he mutters.

'What, then?'

He bungs me a look.

'I'm struggling over whether I'd take someone like you to see a three-year-old daughter of mine.'

He looks back at the road, drives on. Left at the junction, down to the traffic lights.

Red.

We stop, wait.

Rain starts to fall. Hard, gobby drops. Bannerman watches 'em. Hard, gobby eyes. Flicks on the wipers. Lights change. He drives on. First right, second left. Pulls over. I check out the street.

Residential.

Good start. Not a porker joint in sight. But it might still be a trick. Bannerman turns off the engine, twists round in the seat, frowns at me.

'Still not sure why I'm doing this.'

'Maybe you just like me, Pugface.'

'I don't like you and you don't like me. So let's jump over that bit. This information you say you've got—'

'Afterwards.'

'I'm going to need some proof of—'

'Afterwards.' I fix him. 'When I've seen Jaz. And you've let me out again. That's when you get your information.'

'How do I know you'll give me anything?'

'You don't.'

He watches me, narrowed eyes. Then reaches for the car door.

'Wait here.'

'No tricks, Bannerman.'

'Get a life.'

He climbs out of the car, cuts over to number seven. I check the house quick. Two lights on upstairs, one downstairs. I'm guessing there's one porker in there, Fern if I'm lucky. If there's more than one, I got to think again.

He rings the bell, waits.

No answer. I watch, cute as I can. This could go badly wrong. He didn't phone or text ahead. I know that. I've been checking him close ever since we left his house. So whoever lives here doesn't know I'm coming. But I still don't like it. There could be Christ knows how many nebs in that house. And maybe not Jaz at all.

Shadow appears in the glass of the door. I relax a bit. It's a figure I recognize. A bosomy figure. Door opens. And there's DI Fern.

Looks a lot older than the last time I saw her. But that was years ago. Still got plenty up top. And I don't mean her head. Though I'm guessing she's well stitched there too.

Bannerman beckons her out into the street. Another good sign. They haven't gone inside to talk. He's keeping her where I can see 'em, spite of the rain. But I'm still nervous.

I got pictures of Jaz buzzing my head now. They're banging my mind so bad I want to forget everything, dump the risk, jump out of the car, charge in. I'm so close to seeing her again. I can feel it.

But I got to be patient, make myself wait. Cos even if I do go crashing in, what'll that do to Jaz? I scared her once before, scared her terrible. And she's been scared terrible already. I got to hold back or I'll make it worse.

But I'm desperate to get inside that house.

Bannerman's coming back.

I climb out of the car, stand there on the pavement. He walks up, stops, looks me over. Rain's still flicking down. I stare back at him. Hard to read his face. Check past him. Fern's still standing in the doorway, watching.

Hard to read her face too.

Bannerman speaks.

'Come on.'

I follow him up to the house. Front door's wide open. I don't trig through. Can't anyway. Fern's blocking the entrance. Check her over. No weapons, no cuffs. Just a dark look on her face.

Whip a glance past her into the house. Hall stretching straight ahead, rooms off it either side, doors closed. Stairs at the end. Nobody else in sight. She speaks.

'Coat.'

Hard voice. Hard as her face.

Holds out a hand.

'Coat,' she says again.

I take it off, hand it over. She doesn't check the pockets. Doesn't move aside either.

Bannerman shifts on his feet. She glances at him, back at me.

'Just a few minutes,' she says. 'That's all you've got.'

Steps aside, nods me into the house. I check her over again, and Bannerman, and the street. Walk in. Hear the front door close behind me. Stop, check 'em again. Both watching me close. I'm watching 'em back too. But most of me's listening.

For danger.

And for Jaz.

No sound of either. Just the grind of traffic outside the house. Nothing but silence in here. Fern reaches to the left, hangs my coat on a hook by the front door, faces me again.

'You can have it back when you leave,' she says.

I don't answer. I haven't thought that far ahead. Leaving, I mean. All I can see is what I want now. As much time as I can get with Jaz. A few minutes, Fern said. Well, I'll take what I get. And after that?

Can't see anything after that.

Maybe I'll get away, maybe I won't. So what do I care about a coat? They'll cream the blades out of it anyway. Course they will. They got to do that. Bannerman knows I got 'em in the pockets. But what does it matter? What does anything matter?

A few minutes with Jaz.

I'll settle for that.

Fern walks slowly up to me, stops. Talks soft. Not friendly. Just soft.

'She's in the room at the end.'

I turn towards it. Brown door, closed. Not a whisper of noise behind it.

Is she really in there, Bigeyes? Cos I'm full of doubts now. And if she is, do you reckon she's listening to all this? Maybe she can't hear us. Fern talked so soft. And I haven't said a word yet.

I want to call out suddenly, shout Jaz's name, tell her it's me. Tell her I love her. But I know I can't. It's a dimpy idea. It could smash everything. Fern speaks again, soft like before.

'I'm letting you see her for one reason only. Because Inspector Bannerman thinks it might help her. I don't like it and he and I will probably get into trouble for it.'

She frowns.

'But I'm warning you . . . ' She lowers her voice even more. 'If you add one tiny bit more distress to what that little girl has already suffered, then I'll personally—'

'What happened to her?' I mutter.

Fern doesn't answer. Just presses her lips together.

'Tell me what happened to her,' I say.

Bannerman lumbers up.

'We don't know what happened to Jaz.' He's talking as quiet as Fern. 'She hasn't been physically harmed, as far as we can tell.'

'Has she been . . . '

I stop. Can't finish the question. Can't bear to.

But Bannerman answers it anyway.

'She hasn't been . . . interfered with.'

'But she's badly traumatized,' says Fern. 'She's hardly spoken. Just stays silent and closed up, and when she makes any noise at all, it's mostly to cry out in this quiet . . . kind of whimper. And mostly for you. Or Rebecca Jakes.'

I hurry down the hall, stop outside the door, look back. Fern and Bannerman are standing where they were, watching close. I turn back to the door, stare at it.

Jesus, Bigeyes. My heart's pumping. I'm more scared than I've ever been in my life. That's right—scared. Not of what I'm going to find. But of something far worse.

I'm scared I won't be able to make her better again.

I take a breath, reach out, grip the handle.

Push open the door.

34 STEP IN, STOP. One glance is enough. I close the door behind me. Cos I've seen what I want. And I want it all to myself. She's sitting in the corner of a sofa, curled up, all by herself. No one else here. Just me and Jaz.

Looking at each other.

She's got her eyes wide and she's staring. Not talking, not murmuring or whimpering or crying. Just staring, like I'm . . .

I don't know.

Just staring.

She moves, a little shiver of her arm. It's clutching a cuddly thing. Teddy or a squirrel, I think. Can't see cos it's tucked under her. Some part of me's checked out the rest of the room. Window facing the garden. Bookshelves, desk, armchair.

Nothing that matters.

Cos only one thing matters.

'Jaz,' I murmur.

I'm standing like I'm frozen. I don't know how to move, how to make her not be scared. Cos she is scared, Bigeyes. And I can see now what her eyes mean. They're looking for new danger. Cos that's all she's seen since those dronks took her.

And plenty before too.

'Jaz, it's me, baby.'

She squeezes the cuddly thing closer. And now I'm moving. I'm walking over, slow as I can, trying to smile. She's still staring, wide eyes, and now her mouth's opening. I can feel the scream inside it, ready to break out.

I got to stop it.

Or Fern'll smack me straight out of here.

'Jaz, sweetheart,' I whisper.

The scream doesn't come. She's still got her mouth open but she's just watching. I drop down on my knees. I'm close to the sofa now and I can reach her. I stretch out my hand, see her edge back.

'It's all right, Jaz.'

She holds still, fixes my hand with her eyes, watches it draw near.

'It's all right, Jaz. It's me.'

She pulls out the cuddly thing, stuffs it against her chest, holds it tight.

'Squirrel Nutkin,' I murmur.

I stop my hand. Jaz doesn't speak, just goes on watching me.

'I read about Squirrel Nutkin,' I whisper. 'In one of my

235

snugs. And Peter Rabbit. Do you remember him? You used to have a cuddly Peter Rabbit. I carried him for you once. What happened to him?'

She doesn't answer, doesn't show any sign she's understood.

'I must have dropped him somewhere,' I say.

I reach out, stroke the squirrel.

'But you got a better friend now.'

I hear footsteps outside the door. Two sets. They stop. I wait, still watching Jaz, Jaz still watching me. Door doesn't open. But the footsteps don't start again. I can feel Fern and Bannerman out there, listening.

I got to keep 'em out.

Cos I'm telling you, Bigeyes, I won't get this moment back. And there won't be another one after it. I got to talk, make 'em hear something. If there's silence, they'll come bursting in.

'Do you remember that story, Jaz? The one I made up for you?'

Not a word from her. She just clutches the squirrel and stares. I feel Fern and Bannerman fidget outside the room. I hurry on.

'It was a story about Mr Bunny. And this little girl called Jaz. And I never finished it for you. Do you want me to finish it for you now?'

I look at her face. Not even sure she's hearing me. I ease myself onto the sofa, sit still. She doesn't pull back, just goes on staring like before. Again I hear 'em fidget outside the door.

I reach out my hand, slow as I can. Jaz watches it come near, and there's that scream ready in her mouth again. It's in her eyes too. I stop my hand, rest it on Squirrel Nutkin.

'It's all right, Jaz. It's all right. I'm not going to hurt you. I'll never ever do that. I'm just going to sit here and—'

'Blade,' she murmurs.

Her voice chills me. I wasn't expecting her to speak. I was expecting her to scream. I'm still expecting her to scream.

'Blade,' she murmurs.

'That's right, baby. I'm Blade.'

She goes on speaking my name. Soft little voice, no expression. Like it's just a sound she's making, a sound with no meaning. And suddenly it's like the name's lost its meaning for me too. She's just saying it, soft, slow, like it's a little piece of noise.

That's all.

She doesn't know what a blade is. So she's just making a noise. Not even sure she connects the word with me. But I'm wrong. Look at her face, Bigeyes. There's so much in there I can't see. But there's also something I can't miss.

Myself.

Locked in her face.

Locked in my name.

And now in her voice.

'Blade,' she murmurs. 'Blade, Blade, Blade.'

I pull her close, all in one movement, and she bundles into me like it's all she ever wanted. I'm crying now, can't stop it. She's not. She's just closed up inside my arms, quiet again. Stopped talking, just breathing, resting against me.

And I'm going on crying.

Silent too. Not wailing or calling out, just . . .

Crying.

Like my whole life's seeping out of my eyes.

She must feel it. My whole body's shuddering. She's got to know I'm breaking up. Cos I am, Bigeyes. I'm breaking up. There's no part of me left that's whole any more.

I stiffen suddenly.

Door bell just rang. I definitely heard it. And now footsteps outside, heading down the hall. Jaz takes no notice. Just goes on cuddling up. I stroke her hair, her beautiful, beautiful hair.

'Jaz,' I'm whispering. 'Beautiful Jaz.'

But I'm listening too. Sound of the front door opening. Bannerman's voice, then Fern's. Don't catch the answer. But I hear the front door close, then footsteps again.

More than last time.

Lots more.

I breathe slowly out. So it was a trap after all. I half-expected it. Check round the room. I could wig it out the window. Into the garden and round the side of the house. Might get away. But I don't move.

And you know what, Bigeyes?

I never intended to.

Cos all I want's here.

'Little flower,' I whisper to her. 'Just like Becky. Too good for a shit like me.'

She looks up at me suddenly. Like it's a reproach.

'Jaz,' I murmur.

I lean down, kiss her on the forehead, straighten up. She goes on watching me, then turns to face the door.

Cos it's just opened.

And there's a small girl looking in.

35

ABOUT JAZ'S AGE and she's standing there all by herself. Nice-looking kid, shy but friendly. Chestnut hair, brown eyes. Not looking at me.

Looking straight at Jaz.

And Jaz is looking back.

I go on holding her. Sound of rain pattering against the window. The little girl in the doorway flicks a glance behind her—and a hand appears, reaches down, strokes her head.

A woman's hand.

I feel Jaz shift against me, twist round to look better. I don't stop her. Cos I know what's happening now, Bigeyes. It's not a trap. It's something worse.

It's the moment I lose Jaz for ever.

There's nebs out there. I can't see 'em all but I can feel 'em. And I know exactly who they are. Maybe Jaz does too. She's sitting up, staring towards the door, and she doesn't look scared.

Maybe it's the other girl who's making her feel that.

Hope so.

Yeah, it is.

I can tell. They like each other. Both shy, both a bit wary, but they're cute with each other. Long way to go. Yeah, yeah. But who cares, long as it works out. The rest are coming in.

Woman, man, boy about five. Got to be the little girl's brother. Same kind of face, same kind of shyness. It's in the parents too. There's something quiet about 'em, something polite and respectful.

I like these nebs.

Woman bends down, takes her little girl's hand, smiles at Jaz.

'Hello, Jaz,' she says.

Jaz doesn't answer. Woman doesn't seem flummed. Just goes on smiling. Husband comes in with the boy. Tall gobbo, lanky. Takes the boy's hand, bends down next to his wife and the girl.

Smiles at Jaz too.

I feel her move in my arms. She's not pulling away but she's not tucking close either. I don't know what she's feeling, Bigeyes. I can't crack it any more. But I do know one thing.

I know what I got to do next.

I slip my arms from her, edge back against the sofa.

She looks round at me suddenly. I fix her back and smile too, best I can. Her eyes trig over me. She doesn't smile, just watches. I lean down, kiss her again on the forehead.

'I'm Sophie,' says the woman.

I look up, realize she's talking to me.

'This is my husband Rory,' she says.

The gobbo gives me a nod. The woman motions to the kids.

'This is my daughter Melody. And my son Philip.'

I look round at 'em all.

'And you are?' she says.

I see Fern and Bannerman standing in the doorway. Watching me. Message clear.

I look back at the woman.

'I'm a friend of Jaz,' I answer.

I stand up, walk over to the door. I don't look back. But I'm waiting for a sound, praying for a sound. A whimper, a word. My name again. Anything from Jaz.

But she's silent.

I reach the door, stop, look back.

She's watching me, just me. I feel my mouth move, feel Jaz's name whisper inside it. But no sound comes out. The woman called Sophie leans closer to the sofa, reaches out to Squirrel Nutkin.

'You've got a fluffy friend, Jaz,' she says.

She strokes the furry head.

'Melody likes Squirrel Nutkin.'

Jaz takes her eyes from me, looks over at the girl.

And I slip out of the room.

Down the hall towards the front door. I can see the rain streaming down the glass, dark against the night outside. Fern and Bannerman stay close, one either side of me. I don't look at 'em. All I can see is the rain on the door.

Gushing down the glass like the tears on my face.

I don't care if Bannerman sees 'em, or Fern, or anyone. Not now. I hear voices back in the room. The woman's, the boy's, the gobbo's, little Melody's.

Nothing from Jaz.

The rain goes on streaming.

I stop at the front door, reach for my coat on the hook. Fern and Bannerman stay close. They're not blocking the door. I thought they would. But they're staying close. I pull on the coat, feel in the pockets. Knives still there.

I look over at Bannerman.

'You can keep the knives,' he says. 'They're no harm to anyone now.'

'What do you mean?'

'Well, you're never going to use them again, are you?'

I feel the darkness closing over me. It's not the night outside the door. It's the night inside my head. The voices from the room down the hall whisper through it. The rain drums on against the glass. I breathe hard, try to block it all out, but I can't.

Fern speaks. Her voice seems to come from a distant place.

'You asked on the phone about the elderly Irish woman.'

'Mary,' says Bannerman.

He too sounds far away.

I try to speak but I can't. I just see the darkness. And Jaz's face, and Becky's, and now Mary's, all three locked inside it. I know what Fern's going to say. She's going to say Mary's dead.

'She's in a hospice,' says Fern. 'I just heard before you arrived.'

I yank open the front door. Rain slams into my face. The voices down the hall go on. I step into the night, stumble down to the gate. Bannerman catches me up, pulls me round.

'You said you've got information. We had a deal, remember?'

I stare up at him. The rain's blackening his face, like it's blackening everything else. I squeeze the knives in my pockets. Jaz is gone, Becky's gone. In a few short hours, Mary'll be gone too.

What's left for me now?

'Be at your house in an hour,' I mutter.

I turn and blunder off down the street. Bannerman calls after me.

'That won't do!'

'Be at your house in an hour.'

I start to run.

'Running isn't the answer!' he shouts.

I put on speed, pelt through the rain, let the darkness drown me. Bannerman goes on bellowing after me.

36

HIS VOICE IS just as angry later. At the other end of the phone.

'You said an hour! What time do you call this?'

'Do you want what I got or not?'

'It's close on midnight, for Christ's sake!'

'Do you want what I got or not?'

I stare out of the phone box. Rain's stopped but it's still wet outside. Wet and cold and dark. Nothing out there worth anything. Nothing in here either.

I crunch in some more coins.

Taken me ages to get here. Had to watch every shadow. And there's lots of 'em out there, more than ever now the blood's starting to run. The bojos are kicking stumps and Hawk'll want something back. And not just from them but from me.

Me more than anybody.

Porkers buzzing too. Same agenda. They all want me,

Bigeyes. Every single one. But you know what? I stopped caring. Cos I'm spun. That's right. I got zippo left.

I kept telling myself, as I was ducking my way here, that least I've done one good thing. Got Jaz back, got her safe. But when you think about it, even that's a spewer. I mean, how good was that really? If it hadn't been for knowing me, she'd never have been in danger in the first place.

So my helping her counts for dog shit.

Cos here's what it comes to, Bigeyes. All I've ever done is hurt and kill. And now the things I've done are hurting and killing me back. I guess that's how it works. You give it out, you get it back.

Bannerman speaks again, quieter.

'I want what you've got.'

'Where are you?' I mutter.

'At my house. Like you told me to be.'

'What room are you in?'

'Does this matter?'

'What room are you in?'

Bannerman gives a sigh.

'The hall. I'm standing in the hall.'

'Take the phone into the living room.'

'What for?'

'Just do it, Pugface.'

Another sigh, a sound of walking.

'I'm in the living room. Now what?'

'Go over to the bookshelves.'

'Don't tell me you're into reading.'

Jesus, Bigeyes. If only he knew. But I got no time to naff about books.

'Top shelf,' I tell him. 'Far left. City atlas. Great big thing.'

It is too. But we're talking about the Beast, remember. The atlas is never going to be small. This one's got Christ knows how many pages. All the streets and all the suburbs going out miles.

'Got it?' I say.

'Give me a chance.'

Sound of a clink.

'You drinking, Bannerman?'

He doesn't answer. More footsteps, a grunt.

'I've got the atlas,' he says.

'Open it. Page twelve. Keep the thing flat or the stuff'll fall on the floor.'

'What stuff?'

'Just do it, will you?'

A pause. Another clink.

'And put the bloody glass down.'

He takes no notice. I can hear him knocking back. Pouring another one too. But now he's flicking through the papers from Ezi's notepad that I blobbed inside the atlas when I broke in earlier.

'What is this stuff?' he says.

'Read it. I'll phone you back in a few minutes.'

'Hold on. Where are you?'

'Never mind.'

'Give me your number. I'll ring you back.'

'No, I'll phone you.'

'But—'

'Read, you bastard.'

I hang up. Bit of a chance. He might get the porkers tracking the call. But I'm hoping he's too busy reading. I'll give him some time. He needs to take this in. And I need time too. Yeah, Bigeyes. I'm in a bad state.

Got to clear my head somehow, calm down, stay strong. Cos the darkness is still there, outside, inside, everywhere. I go on checking shadows up and down the street.

Muffins so far. Duffs and drunks mostly.

But what about the shadows moving in my head? They're not muffins. I'm telling you, Bigeyes, they're meaner than the meanest grink.

I hope he's reading. Christ, he better be. Trouble is, I kept him waiting for this call, cos I couldn't ring him any earlier, and he's got mad. So he probably tipped a few down him while he was slopping round.

I've given him all I got, Bigeyes. Written it all down on those little bits of paper. Names, scams, companies, banks, all the players I can think of, all the deals I know about. How the bojos get shunted, how the jippy gets moved.

And where it goes.

Accounts, numbers, details.

Everything I can remember.

And something else I've written down. My little cupboards in the old city. Like the bridge over the stream, remember? I've told him where they are. Every single one. And I got lots.

I messed up, Bigeyes. Might as well admit it. Made a big, big mistake when I ran away from Hawk three years ago. I should have just wigged it. Blasted out of the Beast and gone to ground far away. He might just have left me alone.

Probably not, cos he's proud.

But he might have done.

Only I screwed up bad. Took stuff from him, took it away with me, cos I was angry and I wanted to hurt him. Small things, easy to carry, but things he really values. Cos they're priceless. Most of 'em anyway.

Something you got to know about Hawk. He likes to possess. Money, power, people—and beautiful objects. Specially if they've been creamed out of someone else's collection. Or even better—lifted from a public gallery.

He loves having original paintings and artefacts in his secret rooms that only he can ever look at. Knowing the porkers and art experts and gallery curators are churning up the world trying to find 'em.

But I didn't take paintings. Too bulky. I took things I could carry easy. Jewels—dodgy, dangerous jewels that cost lives—and miniature sculptures from China and India and God knows where. Ancient parchments, original letters, a lock of Mozart's hair, stuff like that.

Small things, but worth a mint. Wrapped 'em all up proper so they're snug, then stashed 'em in my cupboards, along with jippy I lifted too.

And there's something else I took.

Something Hawk wants back even more than the stuff

I just mentioned. I shouldn't have touched it. I know that. But it's too late to give it all back to him now. Even telling him where it is won't save me. I've hurt his pride, done him too much harm, plus I took his kid. So my days are numbered.

But maybe—just maybe—I can do one good thing.

Before the darkness finishes me.

I pick up the phone, ring again. Bannerman answers at once.

'Yes?'

'Have you read it all?'

'Yes.'

I can hear his breathing at the other end of the line. It's fast and jerky.

'Is this stuff for real?' he says.

'Yeah.'

'Are you serious? Lord Haffler-Devereaux?'

'Let's call him Hawk.'

'But he's one of the most—'

'I know who he is. Or who you think he is.'

Bannerman takes another jerky breath.

'And these other names . . . Raven, Swan, Swift, Owl, Condor . . . are you really suggesting they're code names for the people you've written alongside them?'

'Yeah.'

'But these are all—'

'Big hitters in their own countries. I know that. Jesus, Bannerman. Don't you get it?' I squeeze the phone tight. 'This is something global. It's a war. Just cos you don't know about it doesn't mean it's not happening. So go and check what I've given you.'

'You've also written Eagle. But there's no name along-side it.'

'That's cos I don't know who Eagle is. I just know Eagle's the one at the top. Don't know which country. But it's someone very high up. I'm guessing royal or presidential.'

Bannerman grunts.

'None of this is proof. And I can't help wondering how you've got hold of all this information. There's loads of it. You're not going to tell me you've been carrying these notes around with you for three years.'

'I wrote it all down today.'

'From what source?'

'From memory?'

'You can't have done. There's too much.'

'Well, I did. I remember stuff, all right? It's how I am. I notice things and I stack 'em in my head. Like all your phone numbers.'

I stiffen. A figure's stumbling towards the phone box. But it's only a duff. He peers through, makes a face. I give him the finger and he staggers off.

Bannerman comes back.

'OK, OK. Let's pretend you've got this amazing mem-ory. That you notice things and remember them. That Lord Haffler-Devereaux really is the Hawk, and this . . . organization exists. And all the other things on these sheets are true. It still doesn't explain one thing.'

'What's that?'

'How on earth do you expect me to believe that a man as dangerous and clever as Hawk would give you access to such information in the first place?'

I stare out of the phone box into the darkness. The duff's now slumped on the far side of the street, staring down at the ground. A shiver of rain dusts the glass.

I bite my lip, bang in some more coins. Talk into the silence.

'Do you know what it's like to be a slave, Bannerman?'

37

HE DOESN'T ANSWER. But I don't want him to. I frown.

'It's like having no being. No body, no mind, no will. You're like a puppet. Your master controls every part of you. Tells you when to live. Tells you when to die. And when to kill.'

I spot a new shadow moving at the far end of the street.

But I go on talking.

'Hawk got me when I was seven. I started off as a bit of fun for him. I reckon you know what I mean. But he soon realized I could be useful in other ways. That's how I got close to him. I found stuff out cos he got careless. He had so much power over me he never thought I could be dangerous to him.'

The shadow at the end of the street stops. I watch it, go on.

'He let me right into his life. Even when I was seven. Don't think he realized I remember everything I see and hear. Or pretty much everything. His tongue used to loosen sometimes. He'd wham the crap out of me, then he'd want to talk. In a dronky kind of way, I think he was trying to impress me.'

Bannerman's quiet at the other end of the line.

Can't even hear him breathing.

'Go on,' he murmurs.

'He just treated me like I was no risk to him. And I wasn't. Not then. I was still living wild, cracking it on the streets with low-life. Hawk set me up in dives round the city. I'd live with pushers and pimps and other scum. People he could contact when he wanted me. And he started to want me a lot.'

'So he'd send someone for you?'

'Yeah.'

'Did you ever refuse to go?'

'Once. When I was eight. But it never happened again.'

'What do you mean?'

'Work it out for yourself, Bannerman.'

He says nothing. I go on.

'Hawk owned me. All of me. That's it. He just never saw me as a problem. He'd let me into his private rooms, show me his secret possessions. Let me sit on the floor while he worked at his desk or chummed with his business friends. None of 'em even looked at me. I was just some kind of toy. A mascot. A kid he was whamming. Dangerous to everybody else. But nothing to them.'

I stop. The shadow's moving again. Heading down the street towards me.

Slow.

I watch it, go on talking.

'So I heard stuff, noticed stuff, and remembered it. The passwords he keyed into his computer, the combination of his private safe, stuff like that. I wasn't looking to use it. I just couldn't help spotting it and remembering it. And all the other things he dropped into my head. It stayed there. And when I ran away, I decided to use it.'

'Why?' says Bannerman.

I don't answer. I'm watching the shadow. It's stopped again, halfway down the street. Not watching me. Don't think so anyway. But I'm watching back.

'Why?' says Bannerman.

'Cos I wanted to hurt him.'

Another shiver of rain against the glass. The duff over the street hauls himself to his feet and blunders off. The shadow doesn't move. I feel the darkness draw round me again.

'He got me too early, Bannerman. I was an angry, dangerous little kid but I was vulnerable, and he was too powerful. He could do anything he wanted with me. And you never knew what it was going to be. Sometimes, just for a moment, I'd start to think he cared for me. He'd talk soft, teach me to read and write, whatever. Then he'd whip me just for fun.'

'Jesus.'

'He liked pain. Giving it. Liked seeing me suffer and knowing I'd still be his. He knew I'd do anything for him. And he was right. By the time I was ten, I was his personal assassin.'

I feel the flashbacks start. I close my eyes.

Open 'em again.

'I'd kill anyone he told me to. It was easy at first. No one suspected a little kid. And I could look tiny and sweet and innocent when I wanted to. By the time the target worked out I was dangerous, he was dead.'

More flashbacks. I push 'em aside, hurry on.

'I only ever killed murderers. Hawk's targets were all people who'd killed one of his men. And I was told to settle the score. But then the other crime joints started working me out. And you and your police mates got a bit wise too. Killing got rougher. I was starting to crack up.'

I stop, breathe hard.

Stare at the pictures in my head.

'I kept seeing the faces of the people I'd killed. Every single one. I still see 'em. I get flashbacks all the time. I'm getting 'em now. Their faces peering at me. I tell myself they were all slime anyway, but it doesn't work.'

'Listen,' says Bannerman, 'you've got to—'

'I started to fall apart. Hawk just gave me another target. I told him I couldn't do it. Tried to run away. Then . . . something else happened . . . '

'What?' says Bannerman.

I stare out at the shadow. It's moving again, down the

street towards me. Stops at the alley on the left, turns into it, disappears.

'What?' says Bannerman.

'Look at the last sheet.'

'Eh?'

'Look at the last sheet.'

'It's a list of names,' he says.

'They're the names of the people I've killed.'

'Are you serious?'

'Every one.'

And I've put Paddy down too, Bigeyes. Case you're wondering. But not Lenny and the grunt. Cos I didn't kill 'em, all right? They fell from the balcony by themselves.

But I'm seeing their faces too.

Along with all the others.

'Look,' says Bannerman. 'You've got to come in to the station. You've—'

'Put down the papers.'

'What?'

'Put down the papers. Look inside the atlas.'

'What's this about?'

'Just do it.'

'What page?'

'The page you're already on.'

Silence while he looks. I stare out into the street. Rain's stopped. No shadows moving. Except in my head.

'Have you found it?' I say.

'Found what?'

'Top of the page. Far right.'

'A small cross,' he says. 'Which I presume you drew.'

'It marks a spot at the end of a graveyard. By an oak tree. Get your spade and go dig. You'll find a tin box with an external hard drive inside. It's a backup drive from Hawk's computer. I took it from his safe when I ran away. There's a slip of paper in there too with the passwords you need. So check out the drive. You'll find it interesting.'

And that's the one, Bigeyes. The thing I shouldn't have taken. Tell you why. Cos it kept Hawk on my trail. But you know what? Now I'm glad I took it. Cos this could sink the bastard. Long as Bannerman follows it up.

There's evidence on that backup drive. Maybe all we'll ever get. It's three years old and Hawk'll have changed computers and files and passwords a hundred times since then. But there's enough on that backup drive to incriminate him.

Tell you how I know. Cos there's no way he'd have sent that many grinks after me if it had only been small shit.

'Go dig, Bannerman,' I mutter. 'And do it quick.'

Peeps in the phone.

I push another coin in. Just one. Don't need any more now.

'I got to go,' I murmur.

'Come to the station.'

'There's no point.'

'There is a point. I promise you there's a point.' Bannerman's talking fast, almost gabbling. 'Listen—you've killed. You've killed several times. And you've got to face up to that and take what comes. But you've got a defence. Are you listening to me?'

'Yeah.'

'You've got a defence. You were in someone else's power. It's possible to argue that to a large extent you were forced to act. You've also now given the police valuable information. So there are mitigating circumstances. You must come in.'

I lean against the side of the phone box.

It's no good, Bigeyes. I'm so tired now. And so scared. I stare into the darkness again, search for the faces. But they're not there. Everything's black now. Just one thing left to do.

'Sorry, Bannerman,' I whisper.

I hang up, plod out of the phone box, down the street to the alley. Stop, check it out. The shadow's halfway down, leaning against the wall at the back of the pub. I shuffle down towards it. The figure stiffens as I draw near.

'You're late,' says Ruby.

38

I STOP, PEER up into her face.

'Didn't think you'd come,' I say.

'Yeah, you did.' She looks me up and down. 'So cut the crap.'

I turn down the alley, make my way towards Mother Grime. I can see the river even from here. She's glowing in the night where the lights from the shore speckle her sick, black body.

I don't check to see if Ruby's following. I know she is. I can feel it, like I can feel her anger, her hatred. Sound of laughter coming from The Turk's Head on our right.

What is it about laughter from pubs, Bigeyes? Why does it always sound unhappy? Maybe it's just me. Cos I'm unhappy, the sound of nebs enjoying themselves makes me feel worse. Maybe that's it.

But it's not. I know it's not. Some laughter's OK. Yeah, yeah. But I'm telling you. A lot of laughter's a cry for help. Not that I'm laughing. No point. I'm just crying for help.

And there's not much point in that either.

End of the alley, stop, wait for Ruby. She catches me up, stops by my shoulder. I feel her looking at me, hard. I don't look back. I can't. Guilt chokes me up every time I see her face.

I stare out over the main road, then beyond it to Mother Grime.

'Well?' says Ruby.

I nod down to the left.

'Fish and chip shop down there. See?'

'What about it?'

'We used to meet there. Me and Becky.'

Tap on my shoulder. Makes me turn my head. Ruby's staring hard into my eyes.

'You look at me when you talk to me,' she says. 'You got that?'

I don't answer.

She whips out a hand, cuffs my face.

'You got that?'

'OK.'

'Go on.'

'We used to meet there. After you told Becky she wasn't to see me again.'

'Cos you were a no good piece of shit.'

I drop my head. She reaches out, jerks my chin up again.

'I told you. You look at me when you're talking.'

This is hard, Bigeyes. I'm telling you. This is so hard. Looking at Ruby's like facing Becky's spirit.

'We used to meet there,' I mumble. 'And it was my fault she started coming.'

I wait for another reproach. But Ruby just fixes me with her eyes. I stumble on.

'I just couldn't cope with losing her. When she told me you said she wasn't to hang around with me again, I just . . . begged her. You know? Begged her not to stop seeing me. She was like . . . the only good thing in my life. I know I was shit. You're right. I was bad. I'm still . . . '

Her eyes go on drilling me. I force myself to keep looking at her.

'She said she'd keep seeing me but only if I tried to get better and stopped hanging about with low-life. She knew I was in big trouble. But she still kept seeing me. We had places where we met when she could get away. But this was our favourite.'

I stare down at the fish and chip shop.

Ruby's hand jerks my face back to meet her eyes.

'We used to meet there,' I say. 'She'd get the bus down. I always used to get there early. I didn't want her hanging around on her own.'

'That supposed to impress me?'

'No, I just . . . ' I shrug. 'Yeah, maybe.'

'Well, it don't.'

I feel a deep pain inside me. I don't know how much more of this I can take. Ruby leans closer.

'Go on.'

'We'd buy some fish and chips, and then come and sit in this alley, and eat and talk. She was everything in the world to me. I promise you. I'd never have—'

I see the anger flare up in Ruby's face.

'Come with me,' I say quickly.

I step out of the alley and turn down the main road. Ruby stays close. I can tell she doesn't trust me. Thinks I'm going to screw my promise and wig it without saying any more. I walk on, slow. Can't walk fast anyway. Not now.

Nothing left.

In my body or my heart.

Mother Grime goes on rippling in the night. Cars passing, smellies, taxis. Still busy, even after midnight. The Beast's more restless even than the old city. Plenty of nebs on the pavements too.

It'll be different in an hour.

And an hour after that.

Cos the Beast never sleeps. Never, ever. But two to three in the morning's about as quiet as the Beast ever gets.

So we walk, and walk, and walk, alongside Mother Grime. Ruby hasn't spoken once since we left the alley. And neither have I. Don't really know what I've been doing, apart from walking.

Haven't been thinking.

Or watching for danger.

None of the things I usually do.

It's like I'm dead, Bigeyes. And that's cool. That's so cool.

Stop. At last.

I turn and face Ruby. She's breathing hard from the walk but the anger and hatred are still bright in her eyes.

'There better be some reason for this walking,' she mutters. Checks her watch. 'It's half past two in the morning.'

I look at her.

'That's the time Becky died. Three years ago. And this is the place.'

I turn towards the river. Bogeybum Bridge stretches away in front of us. Just a few cars and taxis rumbling over it now. Otherwise it's quiet. Almost tranquil.

I start to walk over it, Ruby beside me. And the pictures come flooding back into my head. It's going to be hard to talk about 'em. But I got to try. For Ruby's sake.

And Becky's.

'I was in big trouble.' I keep walking, slow, slow. 'And Becky knew it. I never told her any details. But she knew I was living on the edge. She was always trying to talk me out of bad stuff. She wanted me to come in to her school. There was this teacher she liked—'

'Mr Bristow.'

'Yeah, that's right. She said I ought to ask him about getting an education. Going to school and stuff. She was always going on like that.'

'Get to the point,' says Ruby.

'I was up to my neck in trouble. I'd disobeyed someone powerful and I knew he'd send people after me. I had to run, had to get out of the city, and I knew I couldn't see

Becky any more. I texted her, told her I couldn't see her again cos it was dangerous for her. She texted back, said was I in the alley?'

We reach the middle of Bogeybum Bridge.

Stop.

I walk up to the rail, stare down into the black water.

'What happened?' says Ruby.

39

HER FACE IS set like rock. I take a long, hard breath.

'I made a mistake. Texted back, told her yes, I was in the alley. Shouldn't have done. Told her not to come cos it was dangerous. But she did come.'

'She would have done.'

'Only I'd left the alley by then. I didn't expect her to come out.'

'I told you. She would have done. Cos she was brave.'

'I know, I know. But I didn't realize. I didn't think.'

A swirl of wind catches my face. And pictures from the past swirl with it. Mother Grime whispers below.

'I was heading this way,' I go on. 'I knew there were people hunting me and I wanted to go to ground on the south side of the river for a few hours, while I planned how to get away proper. And that's when Becky caught up with me.'

I hear an engine coming from the north side, turn and stare. Just a motorbike heading towards us. But in my head it fades and I see Becky instead. Running, running, running.

'She was running towards me,' I murmur, 'calling my name. Blade, Blade, Blade. She gave me that name. Did you know that?'

Ruby doesn't answer. I shake my head.

'Don't know how she found me this far from the alley. Must have run everywhere looking. All by herself. Didn't even think of the risk. She caught up with me here. Right here.'

I stare down at the bridge, the rail, the river below.

Motorbike chugs past, disappears. Couple of cars follow.

Silence.

Ruby mutters.

'Go on. Finish it off. Finish me off.'

'They came from the south side. They were in a van. I knew it was danger the moment I saw it. Nobody else on the bridge. Becky didn't even notice. She was trying so hard to talk me out of running away. She wanted me to go to the police and tell 'em what I know. But all I could see was this van. I told her to run. She didn't get it. I grabbed her hand and tried to make her. Then I heard the shot.'

'No!'

Ruby claps a hand over her face. I make to reach out but she slaps me back. I blunder on.

'She went straight down. Where you're standing. I knew she was dead. No question about it. She was dead the moment she got hit.'

Ruby starts moaning.

'No, no, no.'

'I was panicking and the van was whipping in. I knew I couldn't leave Becky. I couldn't bear to. I picked her up and tried to carry her towards the north side. I was desperately hoping more cars would turn up or people or something. But it was still quiet.'

Ruby turns away, leans on the rail, crying.

I walk over, stand by her shoulder.

'It was no good. I couldn't run and carry her too. Maybe I should have stayed and let 'em kill me.'

'Maybe you should have.'

'But I didn't. I heard another shot. It missed but it was close. So I put her down.'

'Bastard.'

'I put her down.' I got tears flooding too. 'And then I ran. The van came on. I saw it over my shoulder. It stopped by Becky's body, two guys got out and heaved her over the rail into the river, then they got back in the van and came on after me.'

'Bastard.'

'But by then I was close to the north side and a couple of cars were hitting the bridge, and the guys in the van couldn't shoot cos of them, and . . . I got away.'

I fall silent.

A taxi rolls past, another, then nothing.

Just Ruby weeping, bent over the rail. And me, watching.

She turns suddenly, blares at me.

'Yeah, you got away! But not my Becky!'

I don't answer. She bustles up, slaps me hard in the face.

'You get to live and I don't even get Becky's body. It don't never get washed up. So I got nothing. And she got nothing. Only not you. Cos you got something. You got your shit life.'

I look down. She's wrong, Bigeyes.

Cos I got nothing too. Yeah, I got my life, but what's my life worth if I got no one who cares about me? And no one I can care about? Cos I want to care. And I did care. Meeting Mary, Jaz, Becky. I did care. You know I did.

Bigeyes?

You know I did.

But Ruby hasn't finished. She slaps my face again.

'Don't you dare look down. You look up at me.'

I look up. And I know what's coming. Her eyes snarl into mine.

'And that same day,' she growls.

'I know.'

'That same day Becky goes missing, I come and find you and ask you if you've seen her and—'

'I know. I lie to your face.'

'You lie to my face. Like the worthless little bastard you are.'

'I know I was wrong.' I look down, look up. 'I couldn't

face it, couldn't face you. I know I was bad. And I'm sorry. I'm really sorry.'

She gives a snort.

'And I just knew you were lying. It was written all over your face. That's why I shouted after you and said I'll kill you if you ever come back. I just wish to God I'd had the guts to carry that out when you showed up at my house.'

She turns away from me and stares towards the other side of the bridge. I watch her for a moment, clenching my fists, then walk up to the rail. She doesn't follow. I check over my shoulder. She's still facing the other way.

A car passes, another, another.

Bridge falls quiet again.

Ruby goes on standing there, crying.

I look back at the rail, reach out, start to climb. The metal feels cold and damp. It's slippery at the top and for a moment I'm scared I'll lose my grip. Freaks me bad, Bigeyes. Cos I don't want to do this the wrong way.

I want to do it right.

But I'm over now. Rail's up against my back and I got my feet snug on the ledge. I'm clasping the metal behind me and all I got to do is let go. I stare down at the black mouth.

'I hate you, Mother Grime,' I murmur. 'But I hate myself even more.'

It's all right, Bigeyes. Don't worry. This is meant to be.

I think of Mary, Jaz.

Becky.

And let go.

Tim Bowler is one of the UK's most compelling and original writers for teenagers. He was born in Leigh-on-Sea and after studying Swedish at university, he worked in forestry, the timber trade, teaching and translating before becoming a full-time writer. He lives with his wife in a small village in Devon and his workroom is an old stone outhouse known to friends as 'Tim's Bolthole'.

Tim has written eighteen books and won fifteen awards, including the prestigious Carnegie Medal for *River Boy*, and his provocative *BLADE* series is being hailed as a groundbreaking work of fiction. He has been described by the *Sunday Telegraph* as 'the master of the psychological thriller' and by the *Independent* as 'one of the truly individual voices in British teenage fiction'.

Tim Boon is one of the UK's most respected
curators within the humanities. He is Director of
Science and author of twenty-five titles. He invests
in history, the sciences, story-telling, and teaching,
taking his passions full into wartime. His articles on
the world's history between and the work done in the
past continues above. He reads and it is helpful.

Tim has written eighteen books and been fitted
over, indicating the it's author Council. Studied
Silver Ave, and has particular. W.H. Course, be has a
had a ... rounding what's work in it, now. He has
devoted to the handing he uses as the author of the
psychological studies, and in the ... that work it so too, or
draws to individual which as times. He use in her

Is this the end for Blade...?

Blade has done all he can. But it's not enough. Men are swarming over the city hunting him. And his enemy is still free.

But Blade isn't finished yet. He has strength in him for one more fight. And it's got to be now. Revenge isn't sweet—it's just necessary.

The thrilling final book in the Blade series.